DEVIL GATE DAWN

By Tim Walker

CHAPTER ONE

The girl's high-pitched scream was a show-stopper. Everyone on the platform looked to its source – a golden-haired girl, her wide-eyed freckled face the very definition of horror, one hand flat against her cheek, the other pointing. George looked past her to the push chair rolling slowly towards the edge of the platform as a train pulled into the station. He shouted something and ran towards it, arms outstretched, flailing in a slow motion grab for the handle as the front wheels tipped over the edge...

GEORGE SHOOK HIS head to rid himself of the recurring image. "I'll be clutching at that offer of early retirement, that's for sure," he said to his reflection in the kitchen window. He sat at the table and slowly stirred the mud-coloured liquid in his Best Dad mug. He had seen too much in his thirty years on the railways. Too many accidents. Too many inquests. Too many bad dreams.

He propped his tablet up against a cereal box, between two pale shafts of sunlight on the kitchen table, tapped on the news icon and selected *Sport* from the drop-down menu. Although one month on, the country was still recovering from the effects of an emotional rollercoaster ride, having finally reached the summit of football - a World Cup Final - after 60 years of trying, only to lose to a lively Columbia. His son, Derrick, wandered in and looked over his shoulder.

"'Steele Follows Alli to Madrid'," Derrick read aloud, and sniggered. "Our two best players have cashed in on a World Cup Final appearance and gone to play in Spain."

"Yeah," George muttered as he picked up the tablet, "after Dele Alli finished as top scorer, he could write his own paycheck. Good luck to them, I say. The weather's better there, and this country's going down the pan. 'Tin Pan Alli' might be a better headline."

Derrick picked up on a common thread between them, "Your mug's always half empty, Dad. It's 2026, not 1926. See the positives – we're ranked second best in the world at football for starters."

George scanned through the e-paper for other news. Speculation concerning the new interim government headed by King Charles III dominated, whilst the cost of living crisis that had ultimately brought down the Conservative and UKIP coalition was relegated to page three. Ignoring his toothache he took another muddy, reflective sip: *Uncertainty in the country, and I'm facing a major life-changing moment.* A more positive news item caught his attention. Britain had survived nearly eight years of being out of the European Union remarkably well, with little change in terms of economic activity. George swiped past a picture of the grinning elderly monarch and settled on an alarmist report from the charity Oxfam.

"Here, listen to this!" he shouted at the back of his retreating son. "It says here that the richest one percent of the population is now worth more than the remaining ninety-nine percent put together. Wealth is now more polarised than ever before between a tiny super-rich elite and everyone else." Derrick shrugged and disappeared to his room. George was left to ruminate on the unfairness of life, and the unnerving atmosphere of disillusionment and uncertainty that hung over the country, like a dust sheet draped over an ancient sofa in a departed relative's lounge.

It was a warm, sunny day on the Runnymede council estate in the village of Langley in East Berkshire. George had lived in the area all his life, and had witnessed the slow urban creep emanating outwards from London, swallowing up villages in its path to provide housing for a seemingly endless growing population. The area demographics had changed significantly since the 1990s and many disenchanted residents had voted on diversity with their feet.

As it happened, all were united in complaining about falling wages and standards of living. When the government continued to push through unpopular privatizations and a divisive Forced Repatriation Bill, there was widespread opposition from civil society and the public, culminating in a mass general election boycott. They took to the streets in a 2025 summer of discontent, showing a unity that alarmed the complacent Government with the scale of anti-poverty demonstrations. Their divide and rule tactics were not working.

George had been a reluctant protestor, but had 'liked' the election boycott Facebook group, and had not voted. Things had now changed, alarmingly so, following a turnout of less than 10% in the recent General Election. This had triggered a constitutional crisis, resulting in the Lord Chief Justice annulling the result as unrepresentative of the will of the people, and calling upon the head of state, King Charles III, to form an interim government of national unity to guide the country towards a new form of democratic representation. The country was now in limbo – waiting anxiously to see what the aging quixotic monarch would come up with.

George turned on a radio podcast on his tablet before buttering his toast.

"…Look, there's little hope for change," a studio guest said, "King Charles is one of the biggest and wealthiest landowners in the country, and would surely protect the interests of the ruling classes."

"Let me bring in our other guest, Mark Davies, from the charity, Shelter."

"Thank you, Peter. I disagree, and feel that he'll grasp his new-found power with the verve and imagination for which he's known, and go about reshaping the country in a positive and dynamic way, championing inclusive politics that actually take account of the needs and opinions of the people." There was a guffaw of laughter from his opponent, who came back with a mocking, "We are reduced to relying on the whims of a septuagenarian king who has lived most of his life in the shadow of his illustrious mother. We now have direct rule by a monarch without any parliament to keep him in check..."

He turned it off. *Politics – a self-perpetuating world of opponents constantly banging their heads against each other for little gain.* A dollop of marmalade plopped onto his hairy, exposed thigh, just below his boxer shorts. He scooped up the orange lump as he stood, pulling his dressing gown around him, and carried his mug and plate over to the kitchen sink.

"Today is the first day of my retirement," he said aloud to his reflection in the window. "What are we going to do for the next thirty-odd years, Georgie boy?" He didn't know the answer but figured it would involve a lot of visits to supermarkets and The George and Dragon. George was still here but his ex-wife Gloria, the Dragon, was gone. It was a silly and irritating joke that had persisted down the pub. At least his teenage twins were still with him, although his daughter, Esther, had recently moved out to 'discover herself' at university. She wasn't far away, in London, and often popped in to check on them. George allowed himself a smile of satisfaction, as he regarded bringing up the kids and getting one of them to university as major life achievements.

Sitting down again, George stared forlornly at a leaflet on the table: *Retirement Planning Seminar*. It had been included with the letter he had received the day before from his former employers, Network Rail, confirming his early retirement package. "Maybe I should go - you never know there might be a few useful ideas," he said to no one in particular. He was startled by the insistent ringing of the doorbell. Not expecting anyone, he tied-off his dressing gown and moved cautiously towards the door and the outline of a tall man through the frosted glass. "What's this now, on this day of days?" he muttered.

"Delivery for Mister George Osborne." The tall, pimply youth with unkempt hair and crooked teeth managed a cheesy grin as he handed over a packet. George checked the name and address carefully, and, satisfied it was for him, thumbed the electronic pad. The young man smiled and said, "Didn't fink the former Chancellor would live in such an 'umble abode!" Used to being teased about his more illustrious namesake, George just growled and withdrew. At the kitchen table he looked at the brown cardboard parcel. Amazon - book size. He opened it. *How to Survive Retirement* - a picture of a cat curled up in a basket by a grandfather clock, next to a pair of grandad slippers. The printed form named the sender as his teenage daughter, Esther Osborne.

He laughed out loud (or 'lolled' as his son Derrick would say). The timing was spot on. Happy that she thought of him, he flicked through the book. He enjoyed reading, particularly history, crime and thrillers, and had a full bookcase in the lounge, in addition to an extensive e-book library. However this novelty book would remain on the coffee table for visitors, to amuse and stimulate conversation, with its colourful and humorous cartoons depicting things retired people get up to: gardening, playing golf, lying on a beach. "Where's paying the bills?" he muttered to himself. He liked it, though, and appreciated the thoughtfulness of his daughter. *Don't spoil the*

moment. I'll call her to say thanks. Although she won't be
awake yet - she's a student.

George peered out of the kitchen window of his council flat, down to the small garden of the ground floor flat below. His new neighbour was hanging out her washing on the clothes line. He gazed with longing at her curvaceous figure. Her long black hair played in the breeze and fell on the back of her floral print summer dress. A black and white cat curled around her shapely brown legs. George dragged himself away and finished tidying up.

"Right. Shopping list. Down to the supermarket and then get ready to meet Dave in the pub. Plenty to do."

Shopping done, George readied himself for the short walk to The George and Dragon. It was a warm day so he selected a loose-fitting short-sleeved shirt and combed his thinning brown hair. He was anxious to know if Dave was going to follow his lead and take the offer of early retirement. They had both joined Railtrack as apprentices straight from school. Following privatisation in 2002 they had been fortunate to have kept their jobs, and transferred to new franchise holders, Network Rail. More than thirty-odd years had passed since then. They were both in their late 50s and not getting any younger. George had made his mind up to go, taking forty percent of his final salary as a pension, but would Dave want to carry on working.

BRIGHT FLASHING LIGHTS and the pinging sound of the fruit machine took George back to his old job in the railway signal room at Clapham Junction. He pictured the wide rail signals display board on which he had conducted many imagined symphonies with his orchestra of switches, levers and coloured lights. *Not any more, I'm retired now*. He was snapped out of his reverie by the arrival of his mate Dave, who plonked down a pint of frothy ale on the curled beer mat in front of him.

"I've given the matter some thought, George, and I think I'll follow your lead and take the offer of early retirement." Dave gulped down a mouthful of the amber ale and wiped the froth from his mouth with the back of his hand. "My overheads are relatively low, I have no debt, and can manage on just under half of my final salary, plus the £25,000 lump sum would come in useful."

"Glad to hear it, Dave," said George, smiling. Their glasses clinked in a toast. "We're well out of it. We're still in our 50s and relatively young. Now we just need to think of what we're gonna do to fill the void. I'm still wide awake at six in the morning, ready to go."

After a minute of silent sipping Dave said, "The way I see it, we could both do with a bit of adventure in our lives. Nothing too fantastic, just something we can plan and make happen. Have you had a chance to think of what you'd like to do?"

"As it happens, my daughter sent me this book called *How to Survive Retirement.* Here, have a look. It recommends having a hobby like gardening or basket weaving, and maybe going on a trip you've always wanted to go on, like to see the pyramids or maybe Las Vegas, that sort of thing. Keep yourself busy or you'll stagnate." Dave chortled as he flicked through the book, "OK, so let's do a quick wish list." George opened the notepad on his phone and tapped a heading on his keypad. He looked expectantly at his friend. "Okay, go," he said. They both threw some ideas around and agreed to discard the unrealistic and fanciful ones.

After twenty minutes of talking, George went up to the bar and bought another round. On returning to the table he said, "Right, there are things we could do together, and a couple of personal things we both mentioned that we'd like to do ourselves. This is what's on the list: 'Take up a leisurely sport such as bowls; go on an adventure holiday; start a transport planning consultancy business; find new girlfriends; rob a bank or post office'. Okay, perhaps the last one is a bit too fanciful and unrealistic. Let's focus on the adventure holiday."

GEORGE GOT UP a bit later than usual the next morning, about half seven when the binmen started throwing the wheelies around outside. He would normally have been at work, but now had to adjust to the rhythms of life on the estate. He had not slept well, dreaming about his retirement options wish list. Flashing images of himself and Dave with stockings over their heads holding up the post office at gunpoint. A massive adrenalin rush followed by twenty years in prison. No thanks. The morning brought a conservative clarity – he felt more inclined to ease himself into a comfortable and hassle-free retirement.

He liked the idea of developing an interest, or hobby, and had always harboured a secret desire to be a twitcher. Birdwatching would allow him to spend more time out of the flat with little stress or disturbance. Realistic and achievable. A lady friend would be nice, but he was not one for internet dating or going to social clubs. That can stay on the back-burner. Over breakfast he made a list of equipment he would need. The front door bell rang and he shuffled to the door and opened it. A bright shaft of morning sunlight temporarily blinded him, and as his eyes adjusted he made out the shapely figure of a woman. Not his charming teenage daughter, Esther, but his new neighbour from the flat below.

George, still in his dressing gown, managed to mumble, "Oh, errr, hi Mrs...err..."

"Just call me Sunny," she smiled warmly. "May I come in?"

"Oh, yeah, sure, please come in, my name's George." He stepped to one side and caught a whiff of sweet perfume as she brushed past, swishing her long black hair as she glanced inquisitively from side to side. She was casually dressed in khaki shorts, a tucked-in black t-shirt and flip flops. George quickly guided her into the lounge, which fortunately he had vacuumed and tidied only a couple of days ago.

"This is nice," she said, without a hint of sarcasm, sitting on the faded red sofa.

"Can I get you something? How about some orange juice?"

"That would be lovely."

Wow, she's comfortably the most attractive visitor for some time, George thought as he shuffled to the kitchen, and set about pouring her a glass of orange juice. Sainsbury's finest, with a few biscuits on a plate. *But what does she want? Did she see me looking at her through the window?* He tied his dressing gown tight, for modesty's sake, and carried the fruit juice glasses and biscuits through to the lounge.

"Erm, sorry for my appearance. I'm having a lazy start to the day," George said, by way of explanation.

"No need to apologise," she smiled, "it's I who am intruding. I noticed you hadn't gone to work, and thought I'd come over and introduce myself properly to you. In a civilised manner, so to speak."

She locked her large brown eyes on him. George was enchanted at her serene beauty; her fine features and smooth coffee-coloured skin. He had not met many Indian women before, and certainly none as attractive as his new neighbour. She elegantly crossed her legs and delicately reached for the glass, her silver bangles jangling.

George clicked into charm mode. "I'm very glad you did. I must admit I had noticed you in your back garden a couple of times. How have you settled in? You've only been here a few weeks, haven't you?"

She put the glass down and said, "Yes, I came two weeks ago with my two children. Ravi is fourteen and starting a new secondary school, and my daughter Dita is ten and still in primary. I've recently separated from my husband and we are going through a divorce. I was lucky to persuade the Housing Association to give me a three-bedroom flat, and here I am."

"Lucky indeed," George said. "Well, I've just taken early retirement, hence my undressed state, and have plenty of time to myself now. I've decided to spend more time on my hobby...erm... visiting nature reserves. I'm a member of the National Trust." He checked himself from saying 'birdwatching' as he thought it might make him look a bit nerdy.

"That sounds wonderful, George. You certainly don't look old enough to retire." Her laughter was like a skylark singing: he was captivated. The day had started well indeed. *Maybe fate is intervening to give me a helping hand with my retirement options.* A smirk played across his face as he closed the door.

CHAPTER TWO

"HERE YOU GO, Son," George said as he put a mug of coffee down on the coffee table. Derrick muttered a "fanks" without looking up.

"Your sister's doing well at uni; she called me yesterday. Says she likes her course and has made some friends." George sat on the sofa and said, "On. News." The wall-mounted flat screen flickered to the BBC News channel. "What's the latest on your efforts to get an apprenticeship?" Derrick's face froze and he slowly looked at his Dad. It was an expression that always reminded George of the boy's mum, Gloria. She had left them when the twins were four years old and returned to Africa to nurse her sick mum. She never came back, leaving an unresolved feeling of abandonment behind her.

"Dad, you're always gettin' at me, just 'cause Esther done well at school and went to uni doesn't mean I'm not tryin'. Somefin'll come up."

"Well, we'll be getting on each other's nerves even more than ever now that I'm retired and will be spending more time at home. If you want to see less of me, then get a job. And by the way, what's that fuzz on your face? You'll struggle to pass an interview looking like that."

Derrick put down his tablet and glared at his Dad. "It's all the fash, Dad, it's a neckbeard, I saw it when me and me mates were binge-watchin' *Big Bro 26*. It's hip. Live wiv it."

George couldn't help himself and kept antagonising the boy. "I've noticed you smoking an e-cigarette. What's all that about? You never smoked real cigarettes; they're for people trying to give up!"

"Chicks adorb them, Dad, they get off on the vapes from e-cigs. It's cool, all me mates do it. I'm off to hang out - later." Derrick got up to leave the room. Ten minutes was the max he could usually stand being in the same room as his dad.

George shouted after him, "I've arranged for us to go next door this evening for an Indian meal with our new neighbours, so can you be home by five, scrubbed and ready to go out, please." The bedroom door slammed shut and George was left alone, sipping his coffee. *Perhaps I'm being too insensitive with the boy. He's clearly missing his sister and his drift towards gang culture may be linked to a feeling of isolation. Add to this the jibes from schoolmates for being mixed race. Come on George, try harder; don't needle him - he needs support and guidance.*

BY THE SIMPLE act of entering his new neighbour's house, George had a sense of passing from his own drab world into one of exotic eastern promise. Sunny ushered father and son into the narrow hallway and introduced them to her son Ravi and daughter Dita. The teenage boys mumbled incoherently, like Amazonian tribesmen emerging from the jungle for the first time. Derrick had carried his tablet, as if glued to it. They swiftly established tech-savvy commonality and ducked into the lounge.

"Phew...that was easy," said George, and followed his host into the kitchen. She wore an apron over a floral pattern summer dress, tied tightly at her narrow waist. George quickly averted his eyes away from peeking at her inviting cleavage when she handed him a glass of juice. He couldn't get over how attractive she was, and held the gaze of her brown eyes for a fleeting moment, noting their delicate almond shape and subtle mascara on her long lashes. She had made an effort to look good, but in a modest way.

"No alcohol or meat in this house, I'm afraid," she said with a smile. "Try my fruit punch."

George was in playful mood: "Mmmm, loverley. Although my liver thinks my throat's been cut. As for no meat... it's long been my ambition to discover a new animal and call it *Quorn*, just to upset the vegetarians."

Sunny gave him a quizzical look and a mocking smile. "It's just snack food; can you help me carry these trays through to the lounge?"

George felt a strange calm as he breathed in the sweet-smelling spices that hung in the air, and listened to the undulating warbles of an Indian female singer coming through the stereo speakers.

"Pakoras, poppadoms, paneer," she said, reminding George of the rhythms of rolling stock at Clapham Junction. "This is Aloo gobi and saag, plain yoghurt, samosas, jasmine rice and mini naans. And there's Kulfi to finish." *Mind the doors please!*

"The only thing I haven't made myself is the yoghurt and these chicken tikka sticks. Yes, there is some meat. I thought it would be too cruel to inflict a full vegetarian meal on you both!" They all laughed and filled their plates, eating in contented silence, until George asked Sunny about the pile of cardboard boxes stacked in the corner of the room.

"Oh, they're uniforms for Woolf's Head Security Services. My brother has a contract to supply clothing. They have the franchise to police the Mercia area. I don't know where that is! I sew on the logos. It gives me some income." She smiled and they continued the meal until nothing was left.

"Mercia's an old Saxon kingdom, dating back to the time of King Alfred in the ninth century," George offered helpfully.

"So why have they brought it back now?" Sunny asked.

"Well, England was divided into four Saxon kingdoms, and I guess those divisions have suited those who have carved up the country into policing franchise areas. There are five in England – four regions plus London – and forces for Scotland, Wales and Northern Ireland. Maybe your brother should bid for clothing contracts with the other franchise holders."

"I'll mention it to him," she said, as she stood up to tidy away the empty serving dishes. The boys had bonded well, finding common ground in computer games. They had eaten quickly so they could return to synchronised thumb-twitching over their game consoles. Dita excused herself and went to her room.

"She's very quiet and enjoys reading," Sunny said of her daughter, as she collected the plates. George helped her clear away the remaining dishes and they chatted in a friendly manner, exchanging details of their lives and relationships. Maybe he would pick up brownie points for being a solid single dad. He had decided that he wanted to make a good impression with this bright, well-organised and attractive lady.

"I never expected to meet such a charming and friendly neighbour as you," George said, wiping a glass with a tea towel. "Next time I'll invite you over for a meal – meat-free of course – at my place." She smiled warmly and saw them to the front door. It seemed the boys had agreed to meet up to continue their game. *A new friend for Derrick who was not gang-related.* George kept this thought to himself. He backed away from her front door and grinned.

"Thanks again and good night."

"That went well," George said to Derrick as they made the thirty-second walk to their front door. "It looks like we've both made new friends." He felt at peace with himself, and practically floated over the threshold in a tranquil daze of wellbeing, still sensing the fragrance of incense. His mind was alert, and he said goodnight to Derrick who headed for the bathroom. George hummed a tune as he made himself a coffee. All was well in this corner of the Runnymede Estate.

HE WATCHED A travel programme and his mind wandered back to his only major overseas trip, to Zambia, in the mid-1990s. Zambia Railways, a state-owned company that had been originally established by the colonial British, had requested a signal expert, and George was approached for the trip. He was in his twenties, single, relatively fit, and at the right stage of development in his career. He would most likely make senior signalman on his return, should the placement go well. It would only be for six months, so why not?

He remembered getting off the BA flight at Lusaka Airport and being struck by the warmth of the air and how bright the daylight was on a February morning. It had been dark and freezing cold in London when he left, but for the next six months it would be t-shirt and shorts weather. He was struck by the dilapidated infrastructure in the capital city – drab concrete buildings, wooden shacks selling vegetables by the side of the road, and battered minibuses dodging large potholes.

The Zambian people were remarkably friendly and very welcoming. They had recently voted out their first President – Kenneth Kaunda – who had finally relinquished control of the country after twenty-seven years in charge since independence from the British in 1964. He had stepped aside with good grace, and there was a mood of optimism, as the country united behind the new ruling party – the Movement for Multi-Party Democracy (MMD). There was much work to be done on training and sourcing funding for repairing or replacing equipment, and he was plunged right into the thick of it with the staggering state-owned Railway Company.

He had met Gloria at a staff party. She was by far the most attractive woman in the room – tall and graceful in a traditional chitengi dress, with a warm smile and flirtatious eyes. She spoke very well, and George was taken by her quick wit and sense of humour. They chatted for half an hour, until George was dragged away to meet the Minister for Transport, but he was able to contact her at her workplace the following day, and they began dating.

George was treated as an expert by his Zambian colleagues, which helped build up his confidence, and before long he was giving opinions to senior management on a whole range of operational issues. He clearly knew more than he had given himself credit for, and his overview of how the British railway system operated was listened to and noted in meetings. He was invited to talk to new recruits, and he visited remote and beautiful parts of the country, along the north-south line of rail. In Northern Province he was shown a monument to a dozen railway workers who were killed by a pride of man-eating lions—one of the many hazards to workers, which also included sickness and death from malaria when the tracks were laid in the 1880s. He would never moan about workers' rights in the UK again.

His relationship with Gloria developed, and when it came time for him to leave after six months, he invited her to come to London. He helped her obtain a visa, and a month later she arrived at Heathrow Airport, to be met by an excited George. She moved in with him and they were married a few months later. Twins arrived some time after their marriage – a boy and a girl – and George revelled in his new role as husband and father. His star was rising, and promotion at work gave them more disposable income and a reasonably good standard of living.

However, Gloria never really got over her post-natal depression, and she increasingly became a recluse in their small council flat. At that time there weren't many Africans in the area. She felt isolated and had few friends. Her unhappiness grew and George was at a loss as how to cheer her up. Finally, she announced that she was going back to Zambia to nurse her sick mother, leaving George with the four-year-old children about to start primary school. He felt a deep sense of loss and failure, but focussed on work and bringing up the kids, helped by his sister and mother. The phone calls became fewer and she increasingly became a distant figure in their lives - they would never meet again.

GEORGE AWOKE FROM a deep and untroubled sleep, feeling fresh, rested and alert. After a shower he wandered through to the kitchen and fired up his tablet. He tapped the Mirror icon and checked his horoscope. *Cancer: A steadying influence around your home draws you closer to loved ones. Emotional scars are healed. Trust your intuition and reach out. Money matters feature prominently in your chart. It is a good time to marshal your resources and budget for a future event.*

He smiled at the positive prognosis and straight away checked his online bank account. He saw that his early retirement incentive payment had dropped in. The amount looked odd and out of place... £25,000. He said it slowly, "Twenty-five thousand pounds," and whistled. Added to the existing balance it gave a new total of £28,496.12. "My current net worth," he said out loud, with a chuckle. "Mystic Meg got it spot on." He made a cup of coffee, opened up a spreadsheet and set about making a budget.

Looking out of the kitchen window at the grey drizzle, he felt content to stay in. "Right, I'll tuck away ten grand for the many rainy days to come, allocate three grand each for the kids and the rest I'm going to spend!" He did a search on outdoor and camping equipment stores, found a well-known company and clicked on their website link. They had a store nearby in Windsor and an extensive online catalogue.

George then spent half an hour identifying and listing equipment to buy for his birdwatching and camping plans, up to the value of two thousand pounds, which he felt was a reasonable budget. In addition to the basics of camping, he included a digital camera with telephoto lens, tripod, remote sensor video camera, head lamp, binoculars, appropriate clothing and camping accessories.

He then called the store and was annoyingly referred back to the website to place an online order. Once this was completed, his thoughts turned to ideas for an epic adventure holiday of a lifetime. He had decided he could spend in the region of seven thousand on this, and then texted Dave to ask if he wanted to meet for lunch. A few minutes later a reply in the affirmative flashed on his screen.

George spent the next half-hour searching for adventure holiday ideas and round the world trip fares within budget. He also gave some thought to how he could approach helping his kids out in the most productive way. In the case of Esther, she was already independent and was sensible enough to manage her own money. It was another matter entirely with Derrick, though. Perhaps he could start with some driving lessons. They both had the new Google ID cards, onto which permits, qualifications and license information were now stored, including driving license details. Hopefully they would both be adding their achievements, as they were accrued, onto their cards. He felt happy and in control, grinning at himself as he combed over his hair in the bathroom mirror. *Now down to the pub to talk it all over with Dave.*

GEORGE SAT AT his usual table in deep reflection, running his thumb up and down the cold pint glass, through the droplets of condensation. He was startled by someone behind him swiping a rigid finger across his throat in a cutting motion. "Ha haa! Got you there!" It was Dave. "No one's safe from having their heads chopped off, have you seen the news?"

"Yeah, I've seen it," said George. "Horrific events in the Middle East. It never seems to end. We won't be going there on our adventure holiday. The news is full of the anti-austerity riots up and down the country. It seems the world is in chaos. All except us. Have you given it any thought?"

Dave sat down opposite and sipped his pint. "Yeah, taking a geo-political approach, it looks like we'll have to head west. Go West young man! North America. East and South look like trouble, so it looks like a trip to the USA. We could do an East to West Coast driving holiday, maybe from Florida to Los Angeles, via Las Vegas, maybe see the Trump Wall, and on to the Grand Canyon. What do you think?"

"Broadly speaking, I'm in agreement with your plan," George said, sitting back, "although with the amount of gun crime in the USA it can hardly be described as 'safe'. The route you propose would be hot and sweaty, and there might be trouble in the area north of the wall. An alternative would be New York, Niagara Falls, then across Canada to Vancouver. A more temperate climate and the people might be friendlier in Canada!"

They both laughed and Dave picked up the thread with enthusiastic zeal. "It may be possible to combine elements of the two. For example, we could fly to New York, drive up to Toronto via Niagara Falls, fly to Vancouver, have a look around, then fly down to Los Angeles." He took a satisfied gulp of his pint and continued. "Then we could do the film studio tours, see Hollywood and on to the Grand Canyon, Las Vegas and fly back from there. My sister-in-law works for a travel agent. I could give her our budget and wish list and see what she comes up with. How much do you think we should spend?"

He sat back and looked expectantly at his friend. George was looking past him, distracted by something happening at the bar. "Well, I've made a budget and...Who's that? Someone just ran out and left a bag by the bar rail." Dave slowly turned to follow his gaze. The quiet was shattered by a deafening roar, followed by a bright flash of light. George flew backwards off his stool, airborne in a slow-motion fall, like in a Sam Peckinpah western, arms flailing, eyes blinded by a blaze of white, ears deafened by the roar of a massive explosion. Glass and beer mats filled the air and a woman screamed. He hit the wall with a thud, banging his head and slumping in an unconscious heap.

CHAPTER THREE

CARDS AND FLORAL tributes to a fallen friend. A heart-shaped wreath with 'Dad' in red carnations. George, leaning on a walking stick, read the funeral cards on the mantelpiece as the room slowly filled with darkly-dressed mourners. Shirley was avoiding him, somehow blaming George for talking Dave into early retirement, planning an adventure holiday and meeting in the pub on that fateful day. Now he was dead. "If it wasn't for you he'd still be here," she snuffled, blowing into a delicate embroidered hankie, looking frail and forlorn in widow's black. George stared dumbly at a picture of Dave in his Railtrack uniform on the sideboard.

It was an accident, a simple twist of fate, apart from the fact that the baby was the innocent victim of negligence. The buggy rolled away from the distracted sister, off the platform edge and into the path of an oncoming train. A traumatised driver put on three months leave. Baby James will never see his second birthday, except as an act of remembrance from the grieving and guilt-ridden family. The tiny coffin was too much to bear. I felt obliged to attend the funeral, although exonerated from all blame. I couldn't be held responsible for all 'accidents' committed by members of the public using the railways. Safety is always our first concern. So says the mission statement...

"Dad, are you alright?" Esther pulled his sleeve until he snapped out of his dream and looked into her large oval-shaped brown eyes.

"You have your mother's eyes," he said, smiling as he took her hand. He couldn't help but admire her. She had grown into a beautiful young woman. She looked like a model in a black minidress, showing off her figure and attracting sly glances from the male mourners. An old school friend sidled up to him.

"Hi George, it's been a long time. Wish we could have met in better circumstances. I hear you had a narrow escape?"

"Ken, you're looking well. Yes, poor Dave, it was a cruel ending, and but for the seating arrangement I'd have been a goner as well. Five days in hospital with minor injuries and they let me go, but my leg hurts like hell where they removed some shrapnel. Are you still in the army?"

"No mate, did twenty years and left to set up my own personal security firm. You know, bodyguarding the rich and famous, that sort of thing." He took an awkward sip of sparkling wine from a narrow champagne flue, tilting his head back. "These glasses are not practical for big-nosed guys like me," he chortled, then checked himself for daring to laugh at such a sombre event. He was shorter than George, but stocky and practically bursting the shoulder seams on his suit jacket.

George suddenly wanted to get his views on the terrorist incident. "Ken, what's your take on the interim government raising the terrorist threat level to critical after these bombings? And what of this terror group, the Anti-Poverty League?"

"Well," Ken took a conspiratorial step towards George and dropped his tone to virtually a whisper, "the military are very concerned about a breakdown in civil order. It seems this Anti-Poverty League have struck a chord with the public. Politics has failed people and it has reached a tipping point. Did you see the polls in this morning's news? The APL have a 60% public support rating, and almost half feel they are justified in using extreme methods to make their point. That's numbers for a revolution, my friend."

George was deeply perturbed and, gathering his thoughts, took a sip from a can of beer he had found at the back of the fridge. "But random acts of murder are not acceptable. Dave, and the bar maid Lil, they were just ordinary law-abiding citizens. The end does not justify the means."

"Oh, I'm with you on that, George. But the last democratically elected government failed in its first duty of care – to look after the interests of the broader community, leading to a vacuum in British politics that these terrorists are now trying to take advantage of to cause fear and instability. We are now teetering on the edge, my friend, of a very deep chasm."

A knife clinked on a glass. George welcomed the distraction. Dave's brother tearfully proposed a toast to his late sibling, and the mood of sorrow notched up in the room as heads hung in silent remembrance. George said a few words about the circumstances of Dave's death, but quickly wrapped it up as the level of sobbing increased. Ken gave George his business card as they quietly filed out of the house. They shook hands on the pavement and Ken said, "Call me, and we'll talk some more. I might be able to find out something about who was behind this bombing."

GEORGE SAT HUNCHED forward at the kitchen table, staring at his tablet screen. Derrick came up behind him and saw the website he was reading.

"Dad! You're not thinking of joining the Anti-Poverty League, are you?"

"Far from it, Son, this is the group who has claimed responsibility for the pub bombings that killed dozens including Dave and almost me. I want to learn more about them. I already have a deep loathing for any group whose name starts with 'Anti' because they are set up in opposition to something, rather than having a positive statement of what they are about."

"Dad, I hope you're not gonna go all *Harry Brown* on me..."

George sat back and looked at his son. "I hardly think I'm cut out to be a vigilante, Son. I've never held a weapon or done active service. But I am angry and would like to see them identified and brought to justice. There are no names of individuals on their website, just a statement of their aims. The police want me to make a statement this afternoon, to see if I remember anything, I guess."

George waited for Derrick to go out and then reached for Ken's business card, carefully studying it before dialling the number. "Hello, Ken Jones Security Services."

"Hi, it's me, George. You said you might have some info on this terror organisation?"

"Oh yeah...kinda busy now George, can we meet for a coffee later on today?"

"Yeah, sure. I'll be in Slough town centre from four o'clock; we could meet in Costa if you like?"

"Okay, fine, see you there at four-thirty. Cheers, bye."

George had some lunch and got ready to go to the police station to give his statement. Maybe he could be of some help. There was a man he had not seen before in a full-length raincoat talking to the barmaid shortly before the explosion. There was a backpack left by the bar rail. He would tell them that and try and give a description. He also made a note of some questions to ask them about this APL group from information he had gleaned from their website, and would press them on what they had found out so far from their enquiries. This was not just something he had seen on the news

25

or read about in the papers. This was personal, and he wanted to know who was behind it.

George's interview was with a Detective Inspector Bob Wilson, who was heading up the investigation. He told them what he could remember, and got nothing in return. Wilson was tight-lipped about the investigation and would not be drawn on possible perpetrators. Afterwards, George wandered down the High Street, found a table in Costa and waited for his friend.

Ken arrived with a purposeful bustle and got straight to the point. "There's a local cell of the APL, and I know the identity of the leader." Ken glanced around and leaned forward, elbows on the Formica table. George asked, "Who is he? ...and do the police know?"

"His name is Tommy Styles and I know him from our active service days. We both did a tour together in Syria. Special Ops. This guy is an ice-cold killer, a good sniper with bomb-making skills. As for the police and the security services, I doubt that their intel is as good as mine."

George sipped his latte and glanced out of the window at shoppers walking by with their plastic bags. Normal, everyday life in the town centre, and he wanted it to stay that way. "Well, if you're right," he said, "this is the guy who most likely planted the pub bomb at the George. Chances are he was involved in the other bombings too and will do it again. It's one hell of a way to make a political point."

"I'm with you there, George. Maybe working together we could find out where they're based and what their strength is, then give the info to the authorities. It's not safe out there anymore and this sort of thing could escalate and quickly destabilise the country." George sat forward. "What have you got in mind? You're the expert Ken, I'm strictly a civilian in these matters."

"Well, I've given it some thought and talked to some of my ex-service mates who know him. One of them hated his guts and has agreed to join me in a surveillance and intel-gathering exercise. We've got an address for him from a contact at the social, so I suggest we start with round-the-clock surveillance to see if he leads us to the group. The three of us can take a shift each. Are you in, George?"

"Yes, count me in. I'm ready to do what I can to identify Dave's murderers and bring them to justice. Tell me what to do." George felt positive and purposeful as he strode to the bus stop. *George - scourge of the terrorists, defender of the innocent, overweight champion of the people.*

PALE YELLOW LIGHT from a table lamp projected the silhouette figure of a man pacing across an upstairs bedroom, hand held to the side of his face, talking into a phone. George kept glancing up from the driver's seat of his car, trying not to spill the sweet milky tea he was pouring from a thermos flask.

"Here, let me do that." Sunny reached across and took the flask and cup from him, like she would from a child. George was happy for her company, but still uncomfortable about bringing her on the secret operation. She happened to be in the house when he had taken a call from Ken about the details of their surveillance op and he had reluctantly answered her questions, swearing her to secrecy.

"Look, he's leaving the house." A man in a grey hoody came out and looked both ways along the street before starting off in the direction of the main road. "I'll follow him on foot, you stay here and wait until I call you or I return, okay?" Before Sunny could answer, George jumped out, turned his coat collar up, and began following the hooded man on the other side of the road, limping slightly as he walked without his stick.

The skies darkened and a light drizzle reduced visibility. George followed the hooded figure at a discreet distance, through side streets and alleyways, into an industrial estate. Wide, open roads here offered less cover for George, and he was relieved when the man finally entered a builder's yard through a roughly-cut doorway in a crude partition wall of corrugated iron sheets. He called Sunny and gave the address, and she agreed to bring the car. Then he turned his back on the entrance and called Ken to report in and ask for instructions. "Ken, it's George..." But that was as far as he got, as he fell to the ground, hit from behind with a heavy object.

DRIP, DRIP, DRIP... George slowly came round. Groggy, his head hurt as he tried to lift it. The light was dim. He had experienced this feeling before, only two weeks ago, when he awoke in hospital. *Am I back in hospital?*

Drip, drip, drip... he tried to move his arms but couldn't. As his eyes slowly adjusted to the dim light he looked down, and saw his hands were tied to the arms of a chair. He tried to move his feet. They were tied too. Looking up he could see he was in a large, empty warehouse, alone. A mood of despair came over him. He was a prisoner.

Drip, drip, drip. *Where was that coming from?* A drop of water splashed into a puddle to his left. Painful though it was, he looked up to see water dripping from a steel girder about twenty feet above him. Small birds squabbled and a shaft of sunlight played against the damp breeze block walls. Apart from the sparrows, he was alone in a large warehouse, tied to a chair.

My mind hummed on neutral as I surveyed the sombre faces in the courtroom, not hearing the repeated question of the solicitor. All eyes were fixed on me, waiting for the next words to tumble out of my mouth. Yes, technically speaking, I was responsible. In as much as I was the duty manager at the time of the accident. Funny word, 'accident'. A random happening. A chance event, as if the gods had mischievously intervened in the affairs of mere mortals. But a baby died and blame has to be apportioned, or absolved. I read the prepared statement, the one given to me by the company lawyers. Then the judge will decide where the heavy burden of blame lies, if anywhere. There are other runners in this race. The young sister, left to mind the baby. The mother, who went to buy cigarettes. It's out of my hands, entwined in legalese and the cold weave of fate...

Just then a noise grabbed George's attention. Terror filled his heart as he recognised the sound – from the movies – of a chainsaw. The buzzing noise was off to his left, out of sight. Then it grew louder and he heard the sound of footsteps approaching. Drip, drip, drip...step, step, step. A blurred figure came into his peripheral vision, moving slowly from his left until he was standing in front of him.

"Fee, fi, fo, fum, I'll soon smell the blood of an Englishman." His muffled voice couldn't hide his accent - that indistinct London overspill. Home Counties poor. Dressed in black trackie bottoms, grey sweat top with the hood up and a plastic pig mask over his face. In his hands was a small chainsaw. Zzzzzzz... George couldn't take his eyes off it.

George gripped the arms of the chair, his body rigid with fear, eyes wide in terror. The man held the chainsaw out in front of him, pointing the whirring edge at his head. He did not add anything to his little verse, and George was not inclined to strike up a conversation. His mind was spinning: *Is he going to question me or just cut me into pieces? If the object of the exercise is to terrify me, it's bloody well working.* George could feel the perspiration on his brow turning cold in the damp, clammy, stale air of the empty building. He remembered standing outside, calling Sunny to pick him up and then...then trying to call Ken. That's all...did he give his location? He must have been hit from behind.

The pigman took a step towards him and George instinctively leaned back, twisting his head away from the buzzing metal teeth just inches from his face. The buzzing noise of the saw filled his ears. Just then a door at the far end of the building flew open, and a silhouette figure stood in the doorway. *Friend or foe?*

A trickle of salty sweat ran into George's eye, making him blink. The chainsaw's teeth were barely two inches from his face and the buzzing noise filled his ears. Terrified, he strained to look past his tormentor to a figure approaching from behind.

"Oi...don't hurt him. I want to ask him some questions." The pigman took a step backwards and lowered his chainsaw, turning it off with a petulant show of annoyance.

"If you'd been two minutes later, I'd have sliced his ears off!" His voice was muffled behind the mask, and he stepped to one side as the new arrival approached. The senior man stood in front of George, a shaft of sunlight behind him, giving his body a radiant glow. George squinted up at the dark outline. He couldn't make out his facial features. He would only recognise him again from his size, voice and distinctive rolling gait.

"Now then," the man said in a quiet but threatening tone, "We caught you hanging around outside. Who are you and what's your game?"

George paused before speaking. "My name's Arthur Smith, and I live round here. I was just waiting for a mate to pick me up, that's why I was on the phone. Then someone hit me from behind. That's all I know."

The man stood with his legs apart and hands on hips. "No, no, my friend. You were spying on us. You were seen peeping through the fence, and my colleague thought that you had been following him. Well, had you?" He leaned forward and slapped George hard on the face. George was stunned by the blow and repeated his denial. "I was just killing time, waiting for my mate to pick me up, honest. I only live up the road, in Cromwell Street."

"Well, if that's the way you want it, I'll hand you back to my colleague here, who's dying to try out his chainsaw on a real, live person. This is your last chance. Why were you spying on us?" The chainsaw fired up again, but George also heard another sound at the same time - a car screeching to a halt outside. The interrogator heard it too and said, "Come on, let's scarper, it might be the Old Bill!" They both ran off leaving George breathing a sigh of relief.

Two people came through the door and ran towards him. George's face broke into a smile as he recognised them. "Ken, Sunny, I've never been more pleased to see anyone than you two. There were two of them, they ran off over there." George flicked his head to his left.

"Alright George, we'll untie you first and then see if they're still here. Are you alright? Did they harm you?" Ken swiftly untied his hands and Sunny bent down to untie his feet.

"You arrived just in time. One of them was going to carve me up with a chainsaw." Sunny gasped at this shocking news, and her look of concern touched George. They smiled at each other, holding eye contact for a few seconds until Ken said, "OK, that's enough schmoozing. You two go to the car whilst I have a quick look around."

Ken expertly searched the building with the aid of a torch, his Browning 9mm ex-service automatic poised and ready in his right hand. Sunny helped a limping George out to the car, filling him in on how she had looked for him and then called the number on the business card she had found in the glove compartment. Ken had answered and came over to search the area, quickly homing in on the disused building. George was profusely grateful for her smart thinking and their timely intervention. *She's a clever girl, and good-looking too*, he thought, as he massaged his sore head.

Ken returned with a few papers he had found. Orders for equipment he thought could be used for making bombs. "I think we should report all this to the authorities and let them take it on from here. Are you up to making a statement?" George groaned, wanting nothing more than to go home for a relaxing bath and a nice steaming hot mug of tea. However, Ken was insistent, and he drove them to the central police station.

All three of them gave detailed statements and were questioned by the detective in charge of the pub bombings case - Detective Inspector Bob Wilson. He was not happy to see George again so soon, and rebuked him for getting involved with dangerous criminals. He was tall, thin and had a sour, almost doleful, expression on his face, like someone who did nothing but attend funerals all day. After a couple of hours, he was satisfied and managed a cautious thanks to them, before issuing another warning to stay out of it. Nevertheless, they had come up with some useful leads and he would take it on from there.

George was happy to get home, and didn't discourage his attractive neighbour from helping him through the door, holding him firmly by the arm. She made him a sandwich and mug of tea, and fussed over him whilst he ate and drank. Once finished, he leaned towards her and put his hand on her slender waist, looking into her eyes.

"Sunny, you're the best thing that's happened to me in a long time. I'd given up on relationships after my ex left, concentrating on work and bringing the kids up. But now I've met you, well...you've re-awakened feelings in me I haven't had for a long time." He leaned forward and kissed her on the lips. She did not resist and put her arms around his neck, drawing him closer. Their tongues touched briefly and she pulled away to say, "It's been a while for me too."

George led her by the hand to his bedroom, apologising for the untidy mess. She helped undress him as his arms were still sore, and then slipped quickly out of her clothes. Soon they were both in bed, kissing, and gently cuddling, as George tried unsuccessfully to control the flinching caused by his aching limbs. He felt deliriously happy, despite the pain.

She discreetly left early in the morning, and George, wearing a grin like the cat that got the cream, sauntered into the lounge in his dressing gown. That had almost been worth being beaten and threatened by terrorists. He had a tune in his head and decided he wanted to listen to it. He spoke to his integrated media system: "Play Bob Dylan's Greatest Hits." The music started at track one, and George commanded, "next," and sang along, not entirely accurately:

> *"Clouds so swift the rain won't lift,*
> *Gate won't close and the railings froze,*
> *Get your mind off wintertime,*
> *You ain't goin' nowhere...*
> *Hmmm-mmmm,*
> *Down into the easy chair!"*

He flopped down into his favourite arm chair, letting his eyes wander around the room. Standing lamp, flatscreen television, photos of the family on the side board. He carried on singing:

"Buy me a flute and a gun that shoots,
Tailgates and substitutes,
Strap yourself to the tree with roots,
You ain't goin' nowhere."

CHAPTER FOUR

GEORGE WAS ANGRY. First they blew up his favourite pub, killing his mate Dave and sweet barmaid Lil, and injured him in the process. Then they tied him to a chair and threatened to cut bits off him with a chainsaw. That ain't nice.

He was agitated and paced around the kitchen. He had searched *Anti-Poverty League*, finding their website, which had the effect of making him more wound-up by their pompous pronouncements after their latest bombing atrocity.

"Listen to this!" he shouted to Sunny sitting in the lounge, "'We, the Anti-Poverty League, accept responsibility for the recent UK pub bombings. It is unfortunate that innocent members of the public were killed and wounded, but we regard this as acceptable collateral damage in our campaign to reduce inequality and unnecessary poverty imposed on the majority of the population who are struggling to survive. Our aim is to create a society free from capitalist control...' I can't read anymore, it makes my blood boil! They don't offer any real alternatives, just negative agitation. The arrogance of them!"

She came through and stood next to him, and he lowered his voice, "they end with, 'We are only seeking to redress the balance and draw attention to their crimes and we say, 'No More!'...'"

His frustrated rant was interrupted by the buzzing and vibrating of his mobile. Ken's name flashed up.

"Hi Ken, what's happening?"

"George, I'm driving up from Portsmouth with an ex-army mate of mine, Stevo. We should meet at the services on the M3 near Guildford. Can you be there in 30 minutes?"

"Erm... 40 minutes from here."

"OK, see you there...on the northbound side, mind. Later."

The phone went dead and George closed down his tablet and looked at her.

"I'm coming," she said.

They hurried to get ready. George switched on his GPS and drove quickly through sparse early afternoon traffic, arriving at the motorway services as the rain started to drizzle. No sign of Ken, so they settled into a booth with a tray of tea and pastries. As George checked the time on his mobile he looked up to see Ken and his friend walking in, scanning the room as if looking out for shoplifters.

Ken broke into a smile as he approached their table. "Hi George, Sunny. This is the ex-army mate I told you about, Stevo. He's agreed to join us." Hands were shaken and seats taken. Ken wasted little time in taking charge of the meeting and producing his file on the APL and Tommy Styles. "Of course, our old mate, Tommy, is only the leader of a small cell of maybe two or three living in this area. The big boss is probably the man who questioned you, and as yet I have no idea who he is."

Ken placed an organisation tree diagram on the table. It was blank except for one photo with a name below: Tommy Styles. "I hope to fill in the diagram as we find out more about them. As you see, we still know very little about who they are, where they are and what their next targets will be."

George spoke up, "So what do you suggest we do?" Ken was waiting to be asked and ploughed on with his military-style briefing. "I think we need to infiltrate their group, and Stevo here has agreed to accidentally-on-purpose run into Tommy and try to gain his confidence so he can join their group. Dangerous, yes, but necessary, as we don't have any other leads to go on."

George and Sunny exchanged quick, anxious looks. "Are you happy to do this?" George asked Ken's comrade. "Yeah, I'm ready to have a go. I'll wear a tracking device so Ken knows where I am and I'll send text messages when I can. Ken's right, there's no other way."

A brief silence followed as they all sipped their drinks. Sunny piped up brightly, "We need a name for our group! How about *The Thames Valley Terminators?*" This lightened the mood slightly and some humorous banter ensued. "Makes us sound like a basketball team!" George said. "How about *The Thames Valley Four?*"

Ken chuckled, "Naaa...too reminiscent of *The Guildford Four* or *The Famous Five*! I think, *The Thames Valley Defence Force.*" "Yeah," said Stevo, "it has a ring to it, and we may add to the numbers in the group as we go along."

And so *The Thames Valley Defence Force* filed out into the gentle drizzle of a grey motorway services car park, shook hands and departed. Ken and Stevo would find their old mate Tommy Styles and put their plan into action. Sunny insisted that George accompany her to her self-defense classes and make a priority of getting fit. They had survived an early skirmish, but needed to prepare themselves for the battles ahead.

THE RED PATCHY carpet, the chipped plywood veneer on the bar, the noisy pay-out of the fruit machine, the ankle bracelet on the girl on a bar stool, the whiff of cheap perfume. Ken took in all the details as he entered the mock Tudor, low-beamed suburban pub. He stood at the bar with Stevo, ordered two pints of Dark Lord Ale and surreptitiously glanced about the place.

"Don't look now, but I think I've seen him," Ken whispered out of the corner of his mouth. Stevo looked past him and nodded. "We're going in, and remember our cover story."

They approached a table with four men huddled around, in the far corner of the pub. Ken put on a friendly smile and caught the eye of one of the men. "Hey, is that you, Tommy? It's been a long time, mate!" An initial look of annoyance turned in an instant to recognition, and then to a welcoming grin.

"Hey! Ken, and Stevo! Long time...it's great to see a couple of my old mates!" Tommy stood up and embraced his two former battalion buddies. He addressed the three sour-looking anoraks sat huddled around his table. Rather than introduce them he said, "Hey guys, let's take a fifteen-minute break. I just want to catch up with a couple of old friends."

They found another table and were soon into reminiscences of their tours of duty – Syria, Afghanistan, Iraq, secret missions in Africa and the Far East. They had all been recruited from their army regiments for special ops and had experienced the adrenalin rush of covert missions to snatch or eliminate hostile targets or rescue prisoners. They talked in hushed tones so as not to be overheard – they had all signed the Official Secrets Act and were not inclined to be boastful outside of their peer group.

Ken found it difficult to draw Tommy on questions about what he was doing now, his interests or hobbies. He told him about his security firm and gave Tommy his card, saying that if he ever needed work, just call. Tommy was grateful and seemed more relaxed after half an hour's chat and a couple of pints. He broke up his other meeting and rejoined Ken and Stevo, to continue the army banter.

Another round of beers later, Tommy was becoming more inclined to talk. "Yer know, I've been drawn into politics a bit, by an attractive young woman I met." He sat back and winked.

"Oh, aye. You always had an eye for the ladies, Tommy," Ken said, keen to encourage him to say more. "Tell us about this lovely lady and her politics."

Twenty minutes later Ken had the woman's name, line of business, town where she lived and the nature of her political interest. She was a member of the Socialist Workers Party and had very strong views on the growing gap between rich and poor – or the wealthy elite and everyone else, as she put it. Tommy had gone along with it and they ended up getting very close. It seemed she had ideas on how to make use of his army skills. Ken had enough to go on.

"It's been great to meet you again, Tommy. Just give me your mobile number and let's keep in touch." They parted with handshakes. Ken drove his black Range Rover through the dark country lanes of Berkshire and dropped Stevo off saying, "I'll try to find out more about this mystery woman and then give him a call to meet again. I'll be in touch."

THE THAMES VALLEY Defence Force met in George's front room. Ken and Stevo sat awkwardly on the brown velvet sofa as the warm afternoon sun streamed through the lace curtains. George stood by the window peering suspiciously along the quiet street, whilst Sunny presented a plate of Indian snack food to the appreciative group.

Ken called the meeting to order and George slumped into an armchair, reaching for a samosa on the way down. "I've created a dossier on our mystery woman. Her name is Dervla O'Callaghan, Irish born and with family links to the IRA. She has lived in the UK for eight years and jointly founded the *Anti-Poverty League* with this man, Peter Morris." He circulated typed fact sheets on each individual with photographs attached with paper clips.

"George, I think this Peter Morris is the man who interrogated you in the warehouse." George looked at the photo and shook his head. "It could be, but I didn't see his face. He stood with his back to the light. Short and stocky. I'd have to see him walking towards me to know it was him."

"Don't worry about meeting him again, George. I've had a call from Tommy and he is keen to keep the contact going. He invited Stevo and I, with partners, to a party they're organising. It's for couples, ideally, he said, so I declined on the grounds that I don't have a partner, and put Stevo forward, with a girlfriend, and he accepted. So my proposal to you all is this... Stevo should go to their party with our only female member, Sunny, posing as his girlfriend."

This bombshell was greeted with silence in the room. George and Sunny exchanged glances and then she spoke quickly just as George was opening his mouth. "That's fine by me. I think it's a good idea." Ken smiled and sat back, but George wanted to have his say. "Hold on a minute. This could be dangerous. What happens if they rumble you and your cover is blown? Have we all given this enough thought?"

Ken moved to close the deal. "I understand your concern, George, but there's really a low level of risk here. They will just be mixing with other guests socially, and will only need to remember their cover stories and stick to them. At the same time, they can pick up bits of information about the APL's future plans, and maybe, if the opportunity presents itself, agree to join their group."

Sunny trained hard in the gym over the next couple of days, and memorised her cover story. She was a British-born Indian with strong views on the oppression of the poor by the ruling elite. She had worked as a cleaner at Eton College and had seen for herself how the privileged classes groom their young for positions of power and influence. Democracy was a sham and there was a need to open people's eyes to the Establishment's agenda of driving down wages to increase profits. Divide and rule, and at the same time gradually eroding people's hard-won rights. She would reflect back to them their own propaganda rhetoric, culled from their website. Also, she was taking a class in karate and was all in favour of using force to make a point.

George fretted and worried in the build-up to the Saturday night party. He was also a little jealous when he saw how beautiful and alluring Sunny looked when dolled up ready to be collected by Stevo. "You don't have to wear a dress that shows all your curves," he moaned. "Can't you tone it down a bit?"

She winked mischievously and said, "Come on George, I want to make a good impression and get them to invite us to join their group. You know that's the purpose of it. Look, here's Stevo now!" The doorbell rang and George glumly answered it. Stevo swaggered in wearing black leather jeans and denim shirt, barely containing his muscular physique, and with his shoulder-length blond hair tied back in a manly ponytail. "You look gorgeous," he said to Sunny, holding her waist and kissing her on the cheek. George's heart sank as he waved them goodbye and good luck.

He had decided not to sit at home worrying and called Ken to meet him for a pint in his new local, The Dog and Partridge. The brutal APL had blown up his favourite pub, forcing him to adopt a bigger, more modern and rather soulless watering hole. As he pulled his coat on he reflected on the dangerous nature of the scheme – the APL were a bunch of cold-blooded killers. Stevo and Sunny would be a couple of lambs stepping into a wolves' lair.

SUNNY TRIED TO be relaxed and calm as she stood on the doorstep, but inside her stomach was clenched tight with fear. "Here we go," she muttered under her breath as she saw the outline of someone approaching through the frosted-glass panel. Stevo squeezed her hand gently and gave her a wink of reassurance.

An attractive blonde in full-length evening dress opened the door. "Hi! My name's Dervla. You must be Steve...Tommy's ex-army friend?" Stevo stepped forward and shook her hand. "Yeah, they call me 'Stevo', and this is my girlfriend, Sunny."

Introductions done, they entered the hallway and were escorted through to the kitchen to be offered drinks. Tommy was on bar duty, and the two former army buddies hugged warmly and got straight into 'what you been up to?' chit chat. Dervla poured Sunny a glass of wine and steered her into the living room.

"Hey everyone, this is Sunny. She's a new friend and I want you all to make her welcome." There were four other couples in the room, all aged between mid-twenties and late thirties, Sunny guessed. She was appropriated by a young couple, and soon was sharing life stories with petite Emma and her African boyfriend, Musa. Sunny gave them her cover story, and noticed Dervla was hovering close by to listen in.

The final couple to arrive were Peter Morris and his wife, Jan. He was a short, stocky, balding man in his forties, and his arrival raised the average age in the room. Sunny tried hard to not stare at him and contain the loathing she felt for the man who most likely had been involved in tying up and threatening poor George with a chainsaw. Words were whispered between

Peter and Dervla, and shortly after she turned the music down and called everyone to come together.

"Peter and I would like to thank you all for coming tonight. We have some new friends: Stevo, an old friend of Tommy's, and his lovely partner, Sunny. Let's welcome them all in the usual way."

To Sunny's relief, this turned out to be a round of applause, and not some weird ritual. Dervla continued, "This is a social, so relax, eat, drink and enjoy yourselves!" The forgettable jazz funk music was turned up and both Dervla and Tommy approached their two guests, inviting them to go into the next room for a quiet chat.

They were asked to take a seat and a few minutes were killed with small talk. Then the door opened and Peter Morris came in. Dervla smiled and stood up. "Well, it's a real pleasure to meet you both, and we want to tell you a little something about a group we're all in." Peter stood beside her and continued, "Yes, Dervla, Tommy and I are in what you might call a group with political aims. We'd like to tell you a bit about it, if that's OK?"

Stevo and Sunny looked at each other, acting a little perplexed. "Errr ...not sure we expected this," Stevo said. "Neither of us are particularly political, but we're happy to hear what you've got to say."

"Alright then," Peter continued. "On the basis that Tommy says you're a reliable and trustworthy guy, I'll proceed. We are part of a group who are agitating for political reform in this country. Our ultimate aim is to achieve an egalitarian republic, where the interests of citizens are safeguarded and enshrined in a constitution. Britain doesn't have a proper constitution, nor a Bill of Rights, and our parliamentary democracy that had slowly evolved over hundreds of years has been suspended due to voter apathy. People want change but don't know how to articulate it or make it happen. We know we're the right people to deliver it."

"The political agenda is dictated by a faceless, wealthy, international elite we could call 'the Establishment'. Regardless of which parties or individuals are elected, the Establishment dictates the political agenda and ensure that Britain remains a tax haven for the world's biggest thieves, crooks, bloody dictators and capitalist scum. They had, for a long time, been able to brainwash the population into believing that this is a democratic country and their vote counts. But not any more. Pandora's box has been opened and we are perfectly positioned to take advantage and guide the country towards a brighter and more equitable future..."

Stevo interrupted, "I agree with the broad sway of what you're saying, but both Tommy and I have served in the Armed Forces and taken the Queen's shilling, defending the interests of the so-called Establishment. I'm not that unhappy with King Charles being in control and seeing where it leads us."

"A good point, my friend. Out of all of us in this room, you two have been conned the most, risking your lives to defend the financial and political interests of a small wealthy elite. They're not even concerned about national boundaries, just making money out of ordinary people's misery, driving down wages and deskilling the jobs market..."

Interrupting him, Sunny asked, "And how do you propose to rectify this situation? Surely change is only possible through electing new political leaders...are you putting up candidates for election?" Sunny had cut straight to the chase.

"We have a number of programmes in play," Dervla responded, "and I think we could use your help, both of you, that is if you're willing to get involved. But that's enough for now; we'll talk in more detail later. It's something for you both to think about whilst we join the rest of the group for a bonding session." She smiled, holding the door open for her guests.

Next door they were playing *The Full Monty* soundtrack, and had just reached 'The Stripper'. The lights had been turned down and as Sunny's eyes adjusted to the intermittent glow from dim flickering fairy lights, she gasped in shock as their fellow guests started to strip off and start writhing on the carpet. Soon sighs and giggles gave way to grunting and groaning. Backsides were rising and falling, bodies squirming in unabated lustful pleasure.

"Come on my dears, let's take our clothes off and join in the fun...its mix and match!" Dervla put her arm firmly around Sunny's waist and guided her into the room.

CHAPTER FIVE

IN THE DOG and Partridge, George and Ken sat facing each other over a small wooden table, staring silently at their pints of beer. George spun a beer mat around between thumb and forefinger, until Ken felt obliged to stop his irritating behaviour. "Come on George, they'll be fine. I expect we'll get a text or call within the hour. Drink up and try to relax."

"You know, Ken, I'm beginning to have second thoughts about this. We did the right thing by going to the police and making statements. That Inspector Wilson told us he would take it on from there, and that we should stay away from dangerous criminals. But now we're courting disaster by sending Stevo and Sunny to infiltrate their group."

Ken tried to put him at ease, "Stevo's experienced in intel work. They're just on a fact-finding mission and, if the opportunity presents itself, they will make a casual attempt at joining their group. As long as they stick to their cover stories, they'll be fine."

George sat back and looked at an old man playing a fruit machine, the noises and flashing lights a deliberate ploy to attract attention.

The signal room was a mass of switches, levers and flashing lights. George pulled with all his might on the stuck lever, knowing that he only had seconds to avert a disaster. Two packed commuter trains were on a collision course, erroneously put onto the same line, and he needed to switch one onto a parallel track. Sweat prickled his furrowed brow as he strained his arms, pulling with all his might. Finally, the lever clicked into place, and he heard the radio crackle, confirming the switch. Halleluiah.

"Earth calling George, where are you?" Ken waved his hand in front of George's face.

"Oh, just reflecting on a crisis averted," George replied, sipping his pint.

"I've been involved in plenty of them," Ken grinned, "both military and domestic! Did I tell you about the time..."

THE RHYTHMIC PULSE of the music and the dim strobe lights made Sunny feel a little disoriented. Dervla guided her to the centre of the room and started to unzip her dress. Sunny flinched and pulled away. She could see the other couples in the room cavorting naked on the shagpile carpet, but her prudish nature and sense of loyalty to George was a barrier.

Just then, Stevo appeared and whispered to Dervla, "I'll take it from here, she's a bit shy."

"Suit yourself," Dervla said stuffily, and took a step back, reaching behind herself whilst holding eye contact with Stevo and dropping her dress to the ground. Stevo couldn't help but admire her shapely body.

"You look great, but if you don't mind, I'll start with Sunny and get her warmed up!"

Dervla smiled and withdrew, turning into the waiting arms of her lover, Tommy.

Stevo whispered to his terrified partner, "Come on, let's get undressed and pretend to make out...we still need to gain their confidence before they'll tell us more about their group."

Sunny dropped her resistance and submitted to being undressed. She then helped him out of his clothes. They found a strip of carpet space and lay down together in a close embrace.

KEN FELT OBLIGED to carry the conversation as the morose George offered little and was content to play with the curling beer mats. "Stevo's a good operator, you know. He's fearless and totally reliable in a bad situation. There was this time we were on a covert op in the Middle East. It was when Kuwait was invaded by the Iraqi army, and we were dropped onto the roof of a five-star hotel to protect the guests. There were a few top Yanks and Brits attending some sort of conference, and we didn't want to risk them being captured by Saddam Hussein's boys. Well, we rounded up the guests in the ballroom and told them we would move them to the top floor to wait for evacuation by helicopter. Just then a group of Iraqi soldiers marched into reception..."

Sunny and Stevo were lying side by side facing each other. He took her hand and put it on his waist and drew her closer to him, kissing her forehead. Sunny was overpowered by his masculine body scent, and found it strangely appealing. He was muscular, tanned, scarred and very attractive. With the bumping, grinding and groaning going on all around her, she was disorientated and totally out of her comfort zone. Stevo pulled her tighter to him, and her resistance melted away as she allowed him to kiss her mouth.

"Sunny's shy, honest and trusting... I don't think she'll be able to keep up the deception." George was still fretting. Thinking distraction was the best ploy, Ken replied, "Come on, George, I'll take you on at the pub quiz machine. I'm a dab hand at general knowledge quizzes; let's see if we can win some money." George slowly got to his feet and joined Ken in front of the machine. The friendly face of Pub Landlord, Al Murray, stared back at him from the illuminated display, sporting an insanely wide grin. "Here we go," said Ken. "Sport – Who won the Champion's League Final in 2004-2005?" George perked up, "That's easy – the Miracle of Istanbul. Liverpool beat AC Milan on penalties." Ken laughed, "Correct! Come on, we can take some money from this machine..."

"Get on top and pretend we're making out!" Stevo manoeuvred Sunny up onto him as he lay on the carpet. Holding her firmly by the waist, he moved her backwards and forwards, both imitating the moaning going on around them. She felt awkward, but acquiesced, and in the dim flashing lights it appeared to anyone watching that they were having sex. Sunny felt guilty about experiencing a sexual thrill, but she was on a dangerous covert mission that involved play acting - the stakes were too high to flunk out. Her mind was telling her, *stay focussed on the objective and go along with it.* Her body was telling her, *mmm but it feels so good...*

KEN RECEIVED A text message from Stevo as they were leaving the pub at eleven. "It's alright George, they're leaving the party, mission accomplished, they'll meet us back at your place at midnight. Let's go."

Stevo was buzzing, still high on adrenalin. "We passed the test, swore an oath of secrecy to their organisation. They've invited us to a briefing on their next mission. It'll be tomorrow evening at Tommy's house. It's the one we staked out last week. I had to pretend I didn't know where he lived."

"Well done!" Ken slapped him on the back, smiling, and clearly happy that the plan was unfolding nicely. George was not so sure, and his attempts to hold eye contact with Sunny were not working. She kept furtively glancing away, but she did manage a half-smile to Stevo when they briefly glanced at each other. Had something happened between them? He wanted to question her on her own.

"Hold on a minute," George said, "this sounds far too dangerous. Why don't we give the information to Inspector Wilson and stay out of it?" He was clearly in a minority of one - Ken and Stevo were pumped up and raring to go. Stevo said, "Come on George, we've done the hard bit, now it's just a case of finding out what their plans are. Once we know their next target, then we can hand the info over to the police."

They were all looking at George, waiting for his assent. "Well, if you're happy to go on, Sunny?" She hesitated before replying, "Yes, of course, let's finish what we started." So that was it. Stevo and Sunny had now joined the terrorist group, the Anti-Poverty League; crazy pub bombers who had killed his friend and nearly killed him. He had started this investigation, and now felt uncomfortable that he was putting his girlfriend in danger. He wanted to hold her, comfort her and be comforted, but she declined to stay the night, saying she was tired and had things to do in the morning. George was left alone. His mind was still alive with unanswered questions and unthinkable possibilities.

He put the kettle on and flopped on the sofa and said, "TV on. News." He saw a familiar face stared out from the screen - Inspector Bob Wilson. "Volume up," he said, leaning forward.

"...we detained the pub bombing suspects in the act of planning their next crime. All I can tell you at the moment is that they are two men of Asian origin and appear to be part of an international terrorist group. That's all I can say right now. We'll keep you informed of developments, but for now it seems that another incident has been averted..."

He had a satisfied smirk on his face, and the camera panned to a man with a blanket over his head being bundled into the back of a police van. George laughed out loud. They had got the wrong men! "Typical of the police - fitting up known suspects," he railed at the flatscreen, "get a quick result, whilst the real perpetrators are still at large, planning another atrocity." He called Ken to let him know and then went next door to talk to Sunny.

George had come to realize how much she now meant to him, after years of self-neglect and loneliness that had simply become part of his day-to-day routine existence. He had now met someone he felt a strong attraction to, a soul partner, someone he really wanted to be with. Surely fate had thrown them together? He must challenge her over what had happened at the party, and find out how strong her feelings were for him. He rang her doorbell.

"Oh, hi George," she said, glancing away after the briefest of eye contact.

"Hi Sunny, thought I come over and see if you'd got over the events of last night."

She took him by the hand and led him into the living room, closing the door behind them. This signaled to George that she was ready to talk. "So, Sunny, I know we haven't known each long, but I have strong feelings for you, and, well, feel a bit uncomfortable, or threatened, even, over you and Stevo..."

"Whoa, George," she interrupted, "there's no me and Stevo. I also have strong feelings for you, and choose you over Stevo any day. Look, he's a handsome man, but we were just role-playing at being a couple. If I seem a little...unsettled...by the party, it's because we had to put on a show of being together, and that involved a bit of kissing and cuddling." She looked at George and waited for his response. "It was dangerous, and I was against you going in the first place. You cozied-up to Stevo and looked a little sheepish when you returned. I thought that maybe you were, you know, going to chuck me..."

She moved forward and put her finger on his lips. "Shhhh, George. There's no way I'd leave you for Stevo. He's an egotistical, narcissistic soldier, good-looking and with a great body, yes, but you're the real man in my life." She pulled him towards her and kissed him on the lips. "Now do you believe me?" she asked, pulling away.

STEVO COLLECTED SUNNY just before seven the following evening. George was much comforted on the state of their fledgling relationship, but also agitated about Sunny joining the Anti-Poverty League terror group, getting too close to dangerous killers, and spending more time in Stevo's company. He stood behind his lace curtains watching them drive off in Stevo's Range Rover. He called Ken. "Yeah, they've just gone off. What should we do?" Ken replied, "You do nothing, George. Just stay home and I'll call you later. I've got a wire on Stevo and I'll monitor his conversations from across the street. It'll be fine. Hopefully, we'll get the details of their next planned bombing. Oh, by the way, Inspector Wilson has been suspended following his knee-jerk arrest of the wrong suspects. I'll be liaising with DS Khan if anything comes up. I'll be in touch."

The line went dead and George stood there in his carpet slippers, staring helplessly at the telephone receiver in his hand. He needed to take his mind off it. Shuffling to the kitchen table, he fired up his tablet. 'Attend to some Essential Life Maintenance', he thought. There were dozens of unopened emails, including utility bills and other demands for payment. He clicked on one from a local garage offering Derrick an apprenticeship. Great! "Derrick!" he shouted along the corridor. No answer. He went outside to the utility cupboard and read the gas and electric meters, putting the readings in on his online account. Job done.

There was an email from Esther. "Dear Dad, I hope you are well and are relaxing after your ordeal and stay in hospital." George chuckled out loud at this. 'If only she knew about the setting up of the Thames Valley Defence Force, the surveillance of a terrorist and his being captured and interrogated at the end of a chainsaw, well, she would have a fit.' He continued reading, "I just want you to know that my exchange visit to Harvard University is going well, and I've made some useful contacts for research purposes. Also, I've got a new boyfriend, Dexter. He's invited me to stay on for another week so I can meet his friends and family. I've accepted. I'm really happy, Dad, and I don't want you to make a fuss. I'll email you in a few days and come over to see you when I get back. Don't worry, I'm making time for revision! Love, Esther."

Too right I'll make a fuss. George got to his feet and put the kettle on. There's always tea. His mind was whirring. *What's she doing? She's got final exams in a few months and now she's swanning around the US of A with some guy called Dexter! Welcome to my crazy world – a retired English railway signalman with an African ex-wife, mixed-race teenage kids, an Indian girlfriend and now a Yank as a potential son-in-law...a cosmopolitan hotchpotch. Diversity's come to town in a big way. Add to this the pub bombing and then getting mixed up with a group trying to take on murdering terrorists. Not quite the early retirement I had planned.*

He wandered back into the lounge to watch the news, and, desensitised to the images of rioting, nodded off, before being rudely awakened by the ringing of the phone. He groped around for the receiver in the now dark room and pressed the green button. "Hello?"

"It's Ken," came the urgent whispered reply. "I'm on that waste ground behind the industrial estate. Something's gone wrong. Both Stevo and Sunny have their hands tied behind their backs and are being pushed out of a car by a couple of guys. One of them has a gun. Can you get over here quickly? I've called DS Khan and he's on his way." George ran down the corridor and banged on Derrick's room door. No answer. He opened the door and looked in. Definitely not here. He grabbed his car keys and flat cap, and ran out of the door, quickly firing up his old Ford Mondeo. Sunny was in danger, he needed to be there.

GEORGE PEERED UP at the stormy night sky through his dirty windscreen. High winds were driving wispy clouds across a pale half-moon. A half-remembered verse from his school days came to mind:

The wind was a torrent of darkness upon the gusty trees,
The moon was a ghostly galleon, tossed upon cloudy seas.

He slowed down as he drove onto a gravel road and after ten minutes saw the blue flashing lights of police cars. Seeing Ken's car, he parked next to it and zipped up his coat as he walked gingerly across the waste ground in search of his friend. He had a flashlight to guide his path amongst the rocks and rubbish strewn on the hard ground. There were no buildings here, just stony ground hemmed in by rocky cliffs.

Ken was standing next to a man in a coat with an upturned collar who he assumed was DS Khan. Ken made a brief introduction and said, "The wire Stevo was wearing went dead shortly before they were bundled into a car. I followed them here. It seems they wanted to test or frighten our friends, because after some words were spoken and a gun pointed at them, they were taken back to the car and driven away. I gave the description and number of the car to the Detective Sergeant and they are now looking for it. I kept hidden so they didn't see me. I thought it best to wait here for the cops rather than follow."

George nodded his concern and rubbed his sore leg in agitation. "So we don't know where they've been taken or what danger they might be in?" Ken tried to calm him. "Look, we don't even know if their cover has been blown. Maybe it was just part of an initiation ceremony to impress upon them the importance of secrecy. For now, I suggest we watch the house they went to and see who comes and goes. Hopefully, Stevo will somehow try to get a message to me. I can't text him in case his phone goes off in front of them."

A baffled George reluctantly agreed to go home and wait. Ken was to return to the house where Sunny and Stevo had gone to meet Tommy Styles. A feeling of helplessness came over him as he drove home. He had no idea what was happening and had no control over the unfolding events. He felt small, a dwarf in a world of giants, a feeling he now shared with the poet Blake:

> As flies to wanton boys are we to the Gods,
> They kill us for their sport.

He sincerely hoped no one else would be killed. Now their decision to pursue a group of dangerous terrorists could have put his girlfriend, Sunny, into mortal danger. He checked in on Derrick who was fast asleep. Feeling anxious and a little morose, he made a mug of consoling hot chocolate and took his tablet to bed.

CHAPTER SIX

ESSIE WAS MAKING the most of her student exchange fortnight at Harvard University. Upstate from New York City, she loved the quaint wooden townhouses in Cambridge, Massachusetts - a new world of excellence, producing America's next generation of leaders. At a sorority party she found herself staring into the clear blue eyes of a tall, well-built, handsome young man. She phased out the background noise and tuned in what he was saying.

"Hi there, and welcome to Harvard. I'm a freshman here, Dex is the name."

"Hi, my name's Essie, from Westminster Uni in London. Nice to meet you."

Their handshake lingered and he guided her over to the punch bowl and poured her a glass.

"What's 'Dex' short for?" she asked.

"Well my parents lacked imagination in calling me Dexter. I mean, my surname's Poindexter. So I became Dex or Double Dex."

They both laughed. A bond was forming. She had done a cursory audit of available male talent, and Double Dex was the stand-out guy. His broad shoulders were explained by his passion for rowing, and Essie told him she had been to watch the rowers at the Henley Regatta, not far from her family home. She was careful not to disclose that she had worked there one summer as a waitress, serving the wealthy patrons in a lavish marquee. Summer jobs helped pay for her education.

"That's impressive...wow, Henley! It's my ambition to row there one day."

Clearly, he was from a large and wealthy family, and someone was involved in the National Security Agency. She didn't catch the details. He laughed when she innocently asked if they would be running a security check on her. They arranged to meet the next day, and she decided to go with the flow and see where it took her. There was always the fallback option of excursions with her group followed by the scheduled departure from JFK Airport.

His family owned an apartment near Central Park, and Dex had arranged a weekend there to impress her. She accepted, and he drove her down in his bronze mustang convertible. White picket-fenced farmsteads with horses running gaily across green meadows whizzed by as they laughed their way to New York City. He stopped on 77nd Street, in front of an imposing stone grey building with the words 'Dakota Apartments' on a plaque on the wall. A valet came running down the stairs to take his car keys. A uniformed doorman helped carry their bags up the steps and she giggled with delight as they entered a big elevator. The apartment was beautifully furnished, with paintings on the walls that looked to her like they might be expensive originals. She was shown to her room by a maid, and marvelled at the large double bed and view over Central Park. She had her own bathroom, and unpacked her modest toilet and make-up bags.

After tea and cakes, he took her for a walk through Central Park and showed her the statue of Alice in Wonderland. A favourite place of mine, he lied casually. She didn't mind. He had made an effort to show her something with an English connection.

"How appropriate," she said. "I'm from the crowded, industrialised end of the River Thames, just west of London. I seem to recall that Lewis Carroll, real name the Reverend Charles Dodgson, created the character of Alice at a lavish Victorian manor house on the upper reaches of the River Thames, inspired by a beautiful garden running down to the river. Same river, but different lives...come on!"

She grabbed his hand and they ran along the path by the pond, laughing as they picked their way past office workers sitting on the grass eating sandwiches, dodging mirror-specked joggers, rounding scissor-legged skaters and past shouting dog walkers. She couldn't remember a time when she had felt such light-headed happiness.

They stopped for an ice cream. He brought her a heart-shaped balloon, and they walked past a fenced-in garden - the Strawberry Fields Memorial, dedicated to former Beatle John Lennon. She released the balloon and made a silent wish as a hazy orange sun set over the lake.

"He lived in our building and was shot dead on the steps to the main entrance," he casually remarked. It had become part of New York City folklore, and another tourist attraction. She was slightly shocked at his almost dismissive reference to the murder of the famous Beatle, an icon of popular music and campaigner for world peace. Hand-in-hand they strolled back to the apartment, and she politely declined his offer to take her picture in the spot where Lennon was murdered.

They were tired after a long day, and had supper in the apartment on a laid-out dining table, prepared and served by the maid, Maria. Dex was the perfect gentleman, flirting but not making a move on her. Should she make a move on him? Maybe not tonight. Spin out the suspense until tomorrow. They kissed warmly on the lips. Goodnight. She retired to her room to catch up with her friends on Facebook before falling into a deep, deep sleep.

Essie tried to talk to Maria as she served breakfast, but she was reticent and would not get drawn into conversation, just answering her questions in non-committal one-word responses. She looked up and smiled at Dex as he sauntered in, looking every bit the heir apparent to some uncounted fortune. He kissed her on the cheek and gave his order to Maria, who was doing her best to be invisible. How many girlfriends had she served breakfast to? Dex grabbed the morning papers, no doubt a learned behaviour picked up from his father, and showed her a picture of a grinning President Trump below the masthead of the New York Times.

After breakfast she persuaded Dex to indulge her with a clothes shopping trip, as she simply had nothing appropriate to wear. If he wanted to introduce her to his family and friends, she wanted to feel comfortable and well turned out. He checked his watch and made a quick calculation in his head.

"Yeah, sure. Great idea! We can squeeze in an hour's shopping before we meet up with some of my friends for lunch. Of course I want you to feel right at home and looking good!" He quickly arranged for his cousin Maisie to meet them at Bloomingdale's store, where he had a credit account, so Essie would have a female companion, as girls usually shop in twos. They laughed at his joke, whilst she secretly hoped she would not clash with cousin Maisie. Outside Bloomingdale's they dodged placard-wielding anti-austerity protestors and were ushered into the bright interior by a muscular doorman.

"Trump will soon sort them out," Dex muttered under his breath.

Cousin Maisie was waiting for them by the perfume counter, and Dex made the introductions. She proved to be a friendly and helpful shopping companion for Essie, who was slightly over-awed by the ladies fashion floor in this prestigious store. She had window shopped in Harrods and Harvey Nics with her friends, perhaps buying a scarf or other modest accessories, but never new designer clothes. Here, she could have her pick, and tried on several outfits before they both agreed on something casual for the day, and a seductive evening dress for dinner. Dex re-appeared exactly one hour later, and was relieved to find them at the check-out. Next stop was lunch at a fancy restaurant where a dozen friends were waiting to meet Dex's new girlfriend. Her confidence was boosted by the new clothes, shoes, and a helping hand with make-up from her new friend, Maisie.

She could not hope to remember all their names, and her face ached from keeping it in a permanent smile. She ate little, picking nervously at the haute cuisine. She made a good impression on his many friends, having novelty value as a mixed-race girl in a white American elite environment. "Esther, but friends call me Essie." She was attractive, confident and British, and lacked the paranoid victim complex often associated with African Americans. She scored highly on likeability and played up to the British stereotype – well-mannered, well-spoken ('gawd, just luerve your accent, honey!'), cultured, educated, friendly and polite. In fact, the consensus was that Dex had done quite well for himself. She was suitably vague about what Daddy did. He was a senior transport consultant. That kept them at bay; a vague and phoney social status indicator to feed their speculation and add to her points tally. Maisie and the girls went to the powder room. She declined the invitation to join them.

Essie leaned over to listen in on Dex's conversation with his pals. College quarterback Brad was leaning forward to make his point: "...the main problem now is not the walls themselves but the tunnels underneath. They're popping up all over the place, and thousands are creeping through every night."

She tugged Dex's sleeve, "What's this about tunnels?"

"Oh, erm, it's the Hispanics – they're now using drilling equipment to make multiple tunnels under the Trump Wall to get into our southern states in huge numbers, even more than through the old wire fence border areas. Criminal gangs are making a fortune and investing in drilling equipment."

"No doubt supplied by US companies," Brad interjected. "And besides, you know the President doesn't like it being referred to as 'The Trump Wall', due to all the negative publicity. It's the *Google Golden Mile* in California, and the *Texaco Alamo* in Texas."

"Surely the border guards can catch them coming out of the tunnels?" she asked.

"Of course, but the numbers are so great, and they'll typically have a dozen tunnels synchronised to open at different locations with hundreds pouring through before they can be contained. It's a numbers game."

"A bit like Tom, Dick and Harry?" They stared at her, not having a clue what she was referring to.

"What's that, honey?" Dex asked.

"Oh," she said brightly, "it's from the film, *The Great Escape*. The prisoners dug three tunnels thinking that the guards might discover one or two, and then they all escaped through the remaining tunnel. I think it was Harry."

"Do ya think the Hisps watched that movie?" Brad asked.

Essie bit her lip, deep in thought. "The word 'Hispanic' troubles me. It's so de-humanising. Like in Europe we say 'The Migrants'. They are real people – the World's poor who've been excluded from the capitalist hog roast and now want a chance of a better life for their children. They're not Hispanics – they're poor people from Central and South America."

Dex fixing her with a killer, and slightly patronising, smile. "Let's get the check."

Dex turned away from his friends and held her hand, lifting his shades and making full eye contact, attracting some 'oohs' and 'coos' from the returning women. He said, rather unromantically, "There's a rally tomorrow to welcome President Trump to New York. I've got to attend as I help out in his campaign team. He's running for a second term, but the Democrats are close in the polls. Would you like to come along? It would only take up half the day, and we can do some sightseeing later."

She willingly accepted, already a captive of his easy charm. Was she becoming his girlfriend? Was there any competition? Perhaps she would find out more from closer contact with his friends. He took her for dinner in one of his favourite restaurants. The *maitre d'* was all over him. She wore her new evening dress and felt at ease, soaking up the admiring looks from other diners, some of whom came over to their table to greet Dex and discreetly enquire after his date. Dex chatted about college life whilst she casually scanned the room. He got onto politics and she tried to remain attentive.

"You know, President Trump was formerly one of our country's most successful businessmen, and has placed a heavy emphasis in his first term on developing corporate America. How much do you know about him? What do the British think of him?"

Essie shrugged and said something about seeing a magazine profile of one of his ex-wives.

Dex ploughed on enthusiastically, "He's gonna continue his mission to turn the USA into one big corporation – Trump America, when re-elected, and we're all on board for the ride!"

In fact, she had read newspaper and magazine articles that were not too complimentary about President Trump's first term. American society had polarised alarmingly between the urban executive elite and the rest. The writer's dark joke that New York had become like the fictional capital city Panem in *The Hunger Games* had carried ominous overtones of social unrest. She could see the resemblance in his circle of friends and diners in the restaurant – the trademark Trump big hair, wide-eyed happy expressions showing intimidating rows of perfect white teeth were everywhere, as if preparing to eat you. A ghoulish cult now surrounded the brash leader.

The wealthy elite and their acolytes were doing well, and they exuded an unshakable confidence, borne of entitlement and a determination to keep their bubble-wrapped world as exclusive as possible. She identified more with rebel Katniss Everdene, and wondered when they would tire of her and make a game of her for their amusement. She chided herself and resolved not to spoil this extraordinary moment in her life. Go with it and see where it takes you, girl. She tuned back in to his sermon on the virtues of Donald Trump, whilst quietly forming her own opinions.

That night it happened. Dex made his move after a light supper and champagne on the balcony overlooking Central Park. She felt like she was in a movie, and fell into his strong arms, freely giving herself to this big, attractive, charming stranger. That she shared few of his beliefs and values mattered not, she wanted him, and that was that. He led her by the hand to the master bedroom, and she giggled at the thought of being in his parents' room. It was an easy, effortless and natural coming together. They enjoyed each other and she fell into a deeply satisfied sleep. Essie and Double Dex... a cartoon romance in a fantasy world.

THE HONEYMOON EFFECT soon dissipated when they arrived at the busy campaign office for Mission: Trump America II – the sequel. She was left with a pretty young intern called Kaydee as Dex and the boys went into a conference room to map out their strategy. She picked up a brochure and read – that is, read between the lines.

Trump was still on an unshakable mission to incorporate every company, institution and citizen into one big money-making scheme. He would resolve the problem of the USA's external debt by simply declaring the country bankrupt, using existing legislation to screw the Chinese and other creditors out of billions of dollars of government bonds. Relations with China were already a little strained, and defense spending had increased, but everyone accepted that high military hardware expenditure helped stimulate the economy. There's nothing like an atmosphere of fear and xenophobia to bring a country together, and with the Pacific fleet on full alert, it all helped generate a sense of togetherness. It seemed that his re-election campaign would be based around the twin pillars of fear and greed.

Trump America II would continue to be a reflection of the president's boorish, stubborn and profit-focussed personality. If some of the little people got trodden on in the process, hell, they were acceptable casualties of a righteous capitalist system, fully supported by Bible-belt Christian evangelism. God's plan for America was a truly utopian capitalist society. Long live Trump America!

"Would you like some coffee?" Pamela's squeaky voice broke her reflection. She blinked repeatedly as she asked the question.

"Erm...yes please, white no sugar." Essie surveyed the large reception area, a flurry of activity, but what were they all doing?

She delved into an article in Time Magazine. Immigration was a thorny and controversial issue. Trump's approach so far could best be described as 'hysterical xenophobia.' He would continue to build the corporate-sponsored Trump Wall along the Mexican border, and stubbornly failed to see the irony in its creation of thousands of jobs for Mexican workers. Relations with Europe and the Middle East had become strained over the refusal to grant visas to Muslims. The damning article went on to say that they continued to turn a blind eye to the brain-drain of liberal-minded disillusioned citizens going across the northern border to Canada. Essie put down the magazine, and wondered if it had been vetted by Party officials before putting it out for visitors to read. Perhaps that's the problem: no one reads anymore.

She checked the time and impatiently picked up a newspaper. Drawing some glances, she flapped the broadsheet pages to signal her annoyance at having to sit there for so long. She was drawn to a report on what was happening outside the urban hubs of prosperity; the neglected shanty suburbs and rural towns that were getting poorer as prices rise and the value of their produce and labour were forced down by greedy corporations. People were already getting restless, and more and more were joining increasingly violent anti-poverty marches. The parallels with what was happening back home in Britain were alarming.

In some states, the National Guard had been permanently mobilised into a standing army and separated from the population in military barracks, as more violence led to more deaths. Essie, who was used to British newspaper reporting, found the sterile, sanitised propagandist news reports shocking in their casual dismissal of casualty figures from what was increasingly looking like a barely-contained civil war. It was happening in the UK, and it was happening here. The people have had enough and are fighting back. The real *Hunger Games* had started.

Dex collected her after a couple of hours and they had lunch at his father's club, before a final helicopter tour over New York and Staten Island. Dex was full of it. The focus of the campaign would be on new malls, military might and a booming economy, whilst putting a positive spin on the declining population. She smiled sweetly and got some great video clips of buildings and the Statue of Liberty for a blitz on social media when she got home. The magical long weekend was nearly over, and her time to return to the UK and her boring revision for exams had come.

Dex parked in the short-stay car park at JFK and they made their way to Departures. As they entered the terminal building a man appeared, seemingly out of nowhere, at his side. Dex introduced him as his uncle's security guard, Mac. They fell into a serious and hushed discussion as they crossed the floor to the queue for the check-in desk, with Esther straining to overhear bits of what transpired between the two men.

"...they want you to go over to England and find out more about..." Mac said, looking around.

A loud flight announcement rudely drowned out their whispered conversation. Dex leaned in to try and hear what he was saying, giving the casually eavesdropping Essie no chance.

"Say that again? They want me to do what?"

He spoke loud enough for her to hear. "Sir, they want you to find out what you can about the British group the Anti-Poverty League. They seem to be growing in popularity and your uncle doesn't want them getting a foothold over here."

"Wait a minute, Mac!" Dex turned slightly away from his companion and between flight announcements, she heard: "...I'm not ready for this, I'm still a college student; that was what was agreed..."

Mac glanced suspiciously at her and took Dex by the arm, leading him away whilst whispering earnestly into his ear. Essie completed her check-in and stood close by at a discreet distance, where she could hear little more than the occasional word or phrase. 'Security risk,' 'find out their names,' 'run checks,' was about all she could make out. By the time they got to Departures, Dex was looking flustered and mildly annoyed.

"What's the matter, honey?" Essie said, putting her hand on his arm.

"Oh, err, nothing, just some advice from my uncle's security advisor here." He slapped his shady companion on the back in false bonhomie. They shook hands and he departed. Mac scanned the crowded departure hall from side to side in a well-practiced manner as he made his way to the exit doors.

Dex put his arms around her and they stared into each other's eyes. She had fallen in love with this big American man, and was failing to hold back the tears at this emotional parting.

"Don't cry, honey," he said with his trademark confident smile, "I've decided to come over and see you in little ol' England. I can take advantage of the same student exchange scheme that you're on. Oh, and by the way, I've upgraded your return flight to first class, so you can travel in style. How about that!"

She jumped for joy and kissed him tenderly, "That's great, Dex! I can't wait to host you and show you around London. When will you come?"

"Oh, in two or three weeks. I'll let you know. If you're free, you can meet me at the airport and escort me to one of your top hotels – probably the Ritz, as that's where members of my family usually stay. It'd be great to see you again. I don't want to let you go, you look gorgeous."

She certainly did, attracting many admiring sly glances from fellow travellers. He held her at arms' length to admire her, smartly dressed in designer clothes, hair and make-up perfect. She looked like a model or actress about to travel in style. One more passionate kiss and she wiggled her way on high heels through the doors of the VIP lounge, glancing back coquettishly, to be welcomed by fawning attendants and guided to a comfortable leather armchair. She was leaving New York in a completely different manner to her arrival, one of a dozen scruffy exchange students, giggling and fooling around.

She missed her friends and could hardly wait to tell them of her adventures and social upgrade with Double Dex. Now Cinderella was leaving the ball, to return to her student digs and the dull routine of cramming for exams, but with golden memories and her heart bursting with pure joy and love for her new man. It had been one hell of an exchange visit, she mused as she sipped a gin and tonic, popping an olive into her mouth as she sized up her fellow first-class passengers.

CHAPTER SEVEN

GEORGE HAD DECIDED to keep his appointment at the hospital the following morning, despite being worried about Sunny. Ken had advised him to go, as he was still staking out the house, in the company of an unmarked police van, and had not given up hope of hearing from Stevo. George had recruited Derrick to accompany him, perhaps sub-consciously wanting to keep his last remaining loved one close. Black clouds had scudded in from the west and it had started to rain as they left the flat and made their way to the bus stop. George hated driving in the pouring rain and parking was a problem, and besides, the bus took them straight to the door.

The female driver leaned forward and battled gamely to steer the bus through the storm, visibility now down to a few feet. Incredibly, and perhaps in part due to her familiarity with the route, they reached the hospital bus stop. "Come on," George nudged a doubtful Derrick, "end of the line. It's only a short dash to the entrance. Let's go." Driving rain and a howling wind greeted the half dozen passengers as they alighted from the bus. "Good luck," the driver remarked grimly.

A passenger screamed as a loud crack of thunder greeted them. Hoods up, they leaned forward into the dark and swirling maelstrom of leaves, branches and sweet wrappers, heading for the red glow of the *Virgin Care Hospital* sign over the entrance. George, reminded of his lines from an amateur dramatics performance of Shakespeare's *King Lear*, started to rail against the elements:

> *"Blow winds and crack your cheeks!*
> *Strike flat the thick rotundity of the World!*
> *Crack nature's moulds that make Man ungrateful!"*

The other passengers gave him strange looks, but Derrick, who had warmed to the play having watched three performances, got in on the act and played the Fool:

*"Come on Dad! It's a naughty night to swim in!
Here's a night that pities neither wise men nor fools!"*

George battled on, the doors of the hospital now in sight:

*"Such groans of roaring wind and rain I never remember to
have heard,*

There's another line that I can't remember, then,

I am a man more sinned against than sinning!"

Exit stage left: they barged in through heavy swing doors and were swallowed up by the warmth and chaos of the crowded reception area. "Thank God for solid buildings like this! This storm is a reminder that against the uncontrolled forces of nature, we are weak and defenceless. You don't get that realism in your computer games!" Derrick grinned and shook the rain off his coat, happy and relieved to be inside and out of the crazy hurricane.

George queued to check in with the robot reception, inserting his Google Card when prompted.

"George Henry Osborne," the female robot chimed, "You have an outpatient appointment at 11 o'clock. You have 560 care credits remaining. This appointment will cost 30 credits. Please go to the Bronze Health Care waiting area and wait until your name is called. Thank you and be well."

They bought hot coffees from a vending machine next to the entrance to the Silver Health Care entrance, where an attractive uniformed attendant opened the door for a couple to enter. Their seats looked comfortable. They entered the packed Bronze area and navigated their way past trolleys of groaning storm victims lining the corridor to the Accident and Emergency unit. George's post-pub-blast wounds needed attending to as some were weeping and others, including his stiff leg, just itched incessantly. "Thank God some semblance of the National Health Service has somehow survived all the privatisations," George muttered as they waited on plastic bucket seats to be seen. Derrick connected to the hospital wi-fi and sipped his coffee in silence.

A TREMBLING SUNNY clung on to Stevo's arm for comfort as her eyes wandered around the high-ceilinged lounge room, settling on the delicately plastered Victorian cornices. Flaking paint gave an air of casual neglect. They had not been taken back to Tommy's house after their traumatic warning at gunpoint, but were now in Dervla's house – the scene of the party and their recruitment into the Anti-Poverty League.

She was still shaken by the events of the previous night when they had been bundled into a car, hands tied behind their backs and hoods over their heads, and taken to a piece of waste ground where they were sworn to secrecy at the point of a gun, in a show of intimidation designed to impress upon them the serious nature of their new organisation's business. It certainly had worked for Sunny, although she was slightly perplexed at the overly dramatic performance of her captors, as if there were conflicting opinions on what to do with them. Thankfully, if some had wanted to eliminate them, they had not succeeded.

Hoods were off and their hands untied, and Dervla gave them tea and sandwiches in her front room. Sunny was a bit more relaxed, but now feeling slightly uncomfortable at the easy banter and general bonhomie between Stevo, Tommy and Dervla. They were very familiar and friendly. In fact, Stevo was so naturally at ease in their company, she wondered if he was really play acting or was actually one of the gang. Doubts were etched into her furrowed brow.

She sought to make eye contact with Stevo, who smiled, stood up and went to stand next to Tommy and Dervla. He looked down at Sunny and said, in a mocking voice, "Sunny, I'm afraid you've been taken in. You thought we were infiltrating the APL to spy on them, but in reality, I've been spying on the Thames Valley Defence Force, and now you're our prisoner. Tommy recruited me to the APL some time before Ken got in touch, and they decided I should hang around with Ken for a while to see how far the bungling police had got with their investigation. The answer we now know is, 'not very far', and the incompetent police arrested the wrong people. Last night's little ruse was simply to fool Ken and the police, who are still watching my house, whilst we were moved to another car and brought here. I'm afraid your friends have no idea where you are and we're now free of surveillance and can carry on with our plans."

If there were warning signs she had not seen them. She was crestfallen. The look of shock on her face caused the others to burst out laughing. She had no idea this would happen, and realised with horror that it had all gone horribly wrong, and she was now alone, a captive of the Anti-Poverty League. George had been right! It was a dangerous game they were playing, and now Stevo has declared himself to be one of the enemy.

Dervla's face changed to one of anger and hate as she turned on her frightened prisoner. "So you and your friends thought you could fool us into thinking you wanted to join our little gang, eh? Well, this isn't a game for children, my dear. We are absolutely determined to pursue our political agenda to achieve maximum impact, regardless of the collateral damage. You'll have to remain here as my house guest. Come on." She grabbed Sunny by the arm and dragged her roughly out of the room.

As Sunny got accustomed to the small bedroom upstairs that was now her prison, the others got to work on planning their next bombing mission downstairs. In the absence of their leader, Peter, Dervla was in charge. "Alright," she said matter-of-factly, "now let's focus on our next job. This one will not be mere pub bombings, but something on a much bigger scale. Its impact will be felt right across the country and will be the tipping point for revolution."

Stevo and Tommy exchanged grins and leaned forward intently as Dervla unveiled the plan to strike at the heart of the Establishment – to bomb the country's centre of government, the Houses of Parliament in Westminster.

BACK HOME FROM the hospital, George showered and changed out of his wet clothes. When the phone rang he jumped up to answer it like a sprinter leaving the blocks. Ken's deep voice had a serious tone to it. "George, some bad news, I'm afraid. The police have just gone into Tommy's house and found it empty. They've slipped away, probably during the storm, and we don't know if Sunny and Stevo's cover has been compromised. Stevo's wire is dead and he's made no attempt to text or call me. His phone seems to be switched off. I'm afraid we've lost them for the time being."

George sucked in air through the gaps between his uneven teeth. "Ken, we've put those two in danger. We should never have gone this far, we should have left it to the police..."

Ken interrupted him, "George, we agreed on this plan of action together, as a group. They were both up for it. The best we can do is a bit of snooping of our own. I suggest we go over to Dervla's house and have a look around. Are you in?"

"Yes, of course. We must do what we can."

"Great, I'll pick you up in an hour. Make a flask of tea and be ready for a lengthy stake-out."

They approached the house cautiously on foot, having parked the car at the end of a dark lane. Ken used night vision goggles to search the windows at the back of the house from their vantage point behind a privet hedgerow. He stopped and focussed on movement in a bedroom window. "I think I can see her. At least it's the outline of a woman with long straight black hair, pacing across a room. Here, have a look and see if you think it's her." He gave the military goggles to George who then spent a whole minute staring at the bedroom window, until turning in excitement to his friend. "Yes! It's her, I'm sure of it! She seems agitated – she must be held captive, or else why would she be alone in an upstairs room? We should call the police..."

"No!" Ken snatched back the binoculars. "We don't know the situation and are only assuming she is being held captive because of her demeanour and location in an upstairs room. We need to talk to her and find out what's happening. The ham-fisted police may only put them in more danger. Stay here and keep watch."

Ken left him to do a search of the garden. He returned saying that there was a ladder in the shed that should reach the upstairs window. He would climb the ladder and try to get Sunny to open a window and tell them what was happening. If she needed rescuing, then they could take her down the ladder and escape. They crept across the lawn with the ladder and positioned it between two downstairs windows. George held the ladder and Ken climbed up and tapped on the window.

Sunny's face showed joy and relief at the sight of Ken perched at the top of a ladder. She mouthed a few words to Ken who climbed down to tell George in a whispered voice, "It's locked, and she's definitely a prisoner in need of rescuing. I need to find something to prise open the window. Wait here." He ran in a crouch across the lawn to the tool shed and returned a minute later with a pair of gardening shears and a shovel. "Right, as soon as the window is opened it might trigger an alarm, so I suggest a quick getaway out the way we came and into the car. No hanging around for hugs and kisses, okay?" George just nodded.

Ken wedged his shovel through the patio door handles to slow their access to the garden. Back up the ladder it took him barely thirty seconds to open the window and quickly help Sunny out as the sound of the alarm filled the air. "Where's Stevo?" he asked. "He's one of them! I'll tell you the details later...let's get out of here!" was her shrill reply. A man's head appeared at the window as they started to run across the lawn, but they made good their escape. George took Sunny in his arms on the back seat and comforted her as Ken fired up his powerful Range Rover and sped off along the country lane in a spray of gravel.

Sunny told them of Stevo's betrayal and the plot to blow up the Houses of Parliament. They drove to George's house, where Ken decided to call DS Khan and arranged a meeting. It was past midnight but he wanted to see them immediately. He gave his address to Ken, and the three of them climbed back into the Range Rover and drove through East Berkshire, south of the M4 motorway, to the village of Datchet. Khan invited them in and his wife, Jasmine, clad in a dressing gown, made tea and toast for the weary group. After listening to Ken's briefing, he made a phone call and then asked Sunny if she had heard any details of their plans to bomb the Houses of Parliament.

"No, I'm afraid not. They just unceremoniously dragged me out of the room and locked me in a bedroom. Look at these bruises on my arm!" There was plenty of sympathy and words of praise for her courage, but thoughts soon turned to the imminent bomb threat.

"The security services will take it on from here," Khan said, "but they will want to talk to you all. Don't discuss this with anyone, not even close family members. Give me all your contact details and stay in your homes. This is going to get a lot worse unless they can be neutralized. My MI5 contact has told me the National Crime Agency has placed their three known leaders, Peter Morris, Dervla O'Callaghan and Tommy Styles, at the top of the Most Wanted list. DI Wilson's suspension hearing is tomorrow. I sincerely hope he gets reinstated, as I feel I'm a bit out of my depth with all this."

"We all are," Ken muttered as he sipped his tea. The threat to Parliament had succeeded in elevating the Anti-Poverty League to the level of notoriety they had sought. They had now put the country on the highest level of security alert, and their aims and objectives would now spill across everyone's online news feed.

"DERRICK! COME OVER here and listen to this." George had turned on the television news mid-morning, after a long lie-in. Derrick shuffled into the room, holding his games console as if it was now a permanent attachment to his hands.

"What is it now, Dad? You know I don't like the news," he whined.

George was listening to a studio interview with the former Leader of the Opposition, Hilary Benn, of the Democratic Labour Party, delivering a stark warning to an excited interviewer: "...and despite repeated warnings from my party and civil society, and against a backdrop of heightening civil unrest, this interim government of supposed 'National Unity' is yet to make any statement on how they intend to govern the country, never mind deal with a growing terrorist threat."

"But Mister Benn, need I remind you that we are in this political vacuum precisely because of the failure of party politics that led to voter apathy and a constitutional crisis..." The smug interviewer sat back as the flustered ex-politician came back at him.

"Yes, we know all that, but now we have a right to know what measures are being put in place to deal with this growing lawlessness, and the various groups sprouting up to encourage anarchy. Furthermore, I don't think we're being told half of what's going on in terms of terrorist threats. Is it safe for us to go anywhere near public buildings?"

"Ha!" George laughed, pointing at the screen. "If only they knew! Do you see that, Son? They are all flapping now and will continue to do so until Bonnie King Charles makes some sort of announcement. We are truly in limbo, while the Anti-Poverty League stirs up a recipe for revolution!"

"Come on Dad!" Derrick wailed. "You're being overly-dramatic, as usual. The terrorists can't win. Soon the new government will get busy. King Charles will sort it all out. Remember his son, Prince Harry, is Head of the Army. You'll see."

'If only he knew,' George thought, knowing he couldn't burden his son with the full story of what the APL were planning.

"Despite being out of the EU, we are still one of the wealthiest countries in the world," Bart droned on, "and this culture of rewarding the rich and punishing the poor..." The picture cut from the studio to images of young men with bandanas covering their mouths, throwing petrol bombs at department stores.

"It's started," George said bleakly. "It's the beginning of the end. People have had enough of food banks and charity hand-outs. This is what it's come down to."

He looked glumly at his son, who also had a look of deep concern on his face.

"Anything wrong, Son? I know I've been distracted with all this..."

"Dad, some of my ex-schoolmates are still involved in that gang I used to hang out with, the Run Posse, up in Slough," Derrick said, "and they're putting me under pressure to join them for a big anti-poverty demo..."

George sat up straight and looked serious, "Son, I don't want you hanging around with any gangs of troublemakers, understand?"

"I'm not, Dad!" Derrick wailed. "You know I'm here most of the time. And now I'm playing a game with Ravi from next door. That's what I'm into."

DERRICK SLIPPED OUT when his Dad went over to visit Sunny, and made his way to the grey, concrete and glass row of shops on their rundown estate. Two of the shops had been smashed in, looted and burned out. His mates were hanging around on the corner. He put up his grey hood as he approached. More than a tribal ritual, it was a response to the CCTV cameras. He wanted to leave the gang, but needed a good acceptable excuse to stop them from coming looking for him and bombarding him with hate messages by text and on social media, as had happened to other drop-outs.

"Alright, boy, where you bin hidin'?" she said, stepping away from the wall to greet him with a mock shoulder punch.

Charly Smith was the leader of the Run Posse, a group of local teenagers who patrolled their turf getting high and looking for trouble. She was a bully, a disturbed tomboy on a mission to hit back at the world. She had found her level organising raids on rival gangs and scoring dope and pills for the gang.

Derrick greeted her cautiously, "Alright, Charly. I've been home looking after my old man. He's just out of hospital and needs me to take care of him, so I'm just letting you know that's why I can't hang out any more…"

"Oh no you don't!" She leaned towards him and grabbed a handful of his sweat top. "We've got a big night coming up, and one of the leaders of the anti-poverty movement is coming to see me, with a bag of sweeties, to tell us what our involvement will be. I want you all here."

A small cheer went up at the mention of 'sweeties'. An amphetamine rush always helped with a rumble. Derrick found a space on the wall and took a drag on an e-cig, realizing that getting away would be difficult. He would now have to hang around and see what would unfold.

"We're expecting a few more to roll in," Charly announced, walking up and down in front of the lolling youths. "Then we'll move out to the Holmes estate where we'll meet our contact and get our instructions. Bats and knives will be required, and we'll pick up some containers of paraffin on the way. Something big's going down tonight, and we'll be a part of it." The group cheered and broke out into excited chatter, as Charly fixed Derrick with a threatening stare.

CHAPTER EIGHT

SUNNY WAS SHAKEN after her kidnap and interrogation ordeal. Fortunately, they had not hurt her, apart from bruising on her upper arms where she had been roughly handled. George's attempts to fuss over her were well received, although it was she who ended up preparing a light meal. They had settled down to eat when George's mobile rang. It was Ken.

"I'd better take this," he said with a note of apprehension.

"Hi George, is Sunny OK?" Ken said. There was background noise like a busy office.

"Yes, Ken, she's fine, and we are both grateful for your military expertise in the successful extraction," he said, falling into Ken's army jargon.

Ken got straight to the point, "I'm at the station with Inspector Wilson and DS Khan."

"Is Wilson back on the case?" George asked.

"Yes, he's been given a second chance. To be honest, I think they need him. They're taking this threat of an attack on the Houses of Parliament very seriously. They want to set up a surveillance op based there and want both of us to pitch in as observers, on account of the fact that we stand a better chance of recognising the main players if they approach the building, even if hooded-up. It would involve sitting in their control room and staring at banks of CCTV screens. Are you up for it?"

The short answer was 'No'. George was less than enthusiastic. He wanted more than anything to spend some quiet time at home with Sunny, her kids and Derrick.

"Erm, do I have to get involved? I'm still getting over my wounds from the bomb blast, and, well, I'm inclined to follow doctor's advice and take it easy for a while..."

Ken slipped into army officer mode, "George, this is just sitting in a swivel chair, eating sandwiches and sipping orange juice. No fieldwork, no excitement. They wouldn't be asking us if it wasn't deemed necessary. For Christ's sake! We're talking about preventing a major incident here! Can you imagine the repercussions if the Houses of Parliament are bombed? Come on, mate. Just one more mission and it gives us the chance to nail these bastards. What do you say?"

Well, put like that, it was difficult for George to refuse. As one of the Thames Valley Defence Force he had agreed to following and infiltrating the terrorist group who had bombed his pub and killed his friend. The job wasn't done. They were still at large and planning more atrocities.

"Yeah, of course. Where and when?"

Sunny gave him a hard stare. She had been keen early on, but now fully realised that it wasn't a game. Her experience of being held prisoner by the APL had shown her that they were psychopathic killers, intent on a path of death and destruction to achieve their political goals.

"George, be careful, and stay in the control room. Don't get drawn into any confrontations with those evil people!" Sunny's warning was ringing in his ears as he packed an overnight bag and got ready to meet Ken. Where was Derrick? He left him a note on the kitchen table and sent a short text message that yielded no reply.

THE STORM HAD seemed to mark the passing of summer, and there was a hint of autumn in the cool air as George waited for a train at Langley station. He had a lot on his mind: Sunny's narrow escape, Dave's death and his injury in the pub bombing, and now the prospect of a second gunpowder plot. He stared out of the window as allotments and caravan parks gradually gave way to warehouses and office blocks as the train pulled slowly into Paddington Station. He noticed small changes – an emphasis shift in the ticket hall away from queuing at ticket windows to self-service machines. Cleaners were now mobile, and engineering works never seemed to end. Change was inevitable, incremental, impersonal, and remorseless. *I'm glad I got out at the first opportunity*, he thought as he jostled his way onto the underground.

George, hands deep in his coat pockets, with bag slung over his shoulder, made the short walk from Waterloo Station to the Embankment, enjoying the crossing over the bridge. He reflected on Sunny's emotional account of the act of betrayal by Stevo, and how Ken had grimaced in pain at the thought of his ex-army buddy working for the enemy. Glancing up at the Houses of Parliament in front of him, he was reminded of the picture on the label of a bottle of HP Sauce, and a poem by William Blake whom he had studied as part of an online English lit course:

'I wander through each chartered street.
Near where the chartered Thames does flow
And mark in every face I meet
Marks of weakness, marks of woe.'

He trotted down the stone steps to the Embankment and dodged lines of Romanian women in head scarves, some with kids, rattling tins and crying out in their native language. London had always been a safe haven for refugees but had attracted thousands of economic migrants, many from Eastern Europe, before Britain's exit from the European Union, following a third referendum in 2020. Efforts to repatriate most of the 'economically unproductive' had proved only partially successful, and those who stayed behind had added another layer of colour to the pastiche of London life. George could not help thinking that the old poets would grimace if they came back and saw that begging, homelessness and poverty still exists in an otherwise affluent city. No wonder there was revolution in the air, and the APL planned to light the powder keg.

Ken was leaning over the stone wall and gazing down into the murky brown water as it flowed under Westminster Bridge. "Hello George." They shook hands and walked along in the direction of the Houses of Parliament. George listened silently to his friend, anxious to find out if there were any new developments concerning the terror plot and the traitor, Stevo.

Ken was in an expansive mood, "Did you know that the Houses of Parliament, otherwise known as the Palace of Westminster, incorporates the Great Hall built by the Norman king William II in 1099? It is one of the oldest structures in this city, and now the APL want to make a point by blowing it up. Where Guy Fawkes failed in 1605 with the Gunpowder Plot, they now fancy their chances. Mind you, security is much tighter and high tech these days...I'm sure others have tried and failed and it's been hushed up by the security services."

"The Gunpowder Plot was about religious persecution," George replied. "The Catholics rebelled against a new Protestant nation, hoping to start a revolt. Now, it's about the poor rebelling against the rich. At least, that's the political agenda of the Anti-Poverty League, although I think the cause is secondary to their desire to provoke a bloody revolution at any cost. What do they hope to gain from the fallout, should they succeed?"

"They won't succeed," Ken said. They both lapsed into silence as a stinking dredger loaded with mud and excrement chugged by along the dirty river. George continued his William Blake poem out loud, for Ken's benefit:

*"In every cry of every Man,
In every Infant's cry of fear,
In every voice; in every ban,
The mind-forged manacles I hear."*

"You what?" said Ken.

"That's what William Blake said two hundred years ago about this oppressive, exploitative city of power, poverty and greed. Maybe they should succeed."

Ken eyed his moody companion and said, "Come on George, I've arranged for us to meet the Inspector at the staff entrance to the parliament building. We can play our part in preventing this madness by identifying any of the main activists on CCTV if they approach the building. We should be able to recognise Stevo and Tommy by their body shape and gait long before any of the coppers, even with hoods up. Come on, it's the final act of the Thames Valley Defence Force. Let's finish what we started."

THEY MET WILSON and Khan at the security checkpoint. Ken couldn't resist a subtle dig at the un-suspended Wilson.

"All quiet and not a Muslim in sight."

"Erm, excuse me," DS Khan said, eying Ken with a tired 'here-we-go-again' look.

Wilson gave Ken a peeved look and said, "You should mind what you say, otherwise you'll be the one causing offence. Shall we get on?" They were ushered into the warm security room, with banks of monitors around the walls, and keyboard controls and microphones dominating the worktops. George settled in a comfortable armchair as Ken went on a tour of the building – The Gunpowder Tour, as his jovial guide put it.

Some hours passed as George fiddled with his ID badge, got used to wearing a bullet and blast-proof vest and to the pattern of people coming and going on the monitors through the four main entrances. Suddenly he froze as he recognised the familiar gait of Stevo. His head was covered by a grey hooded top, but it was definitely him. Muscular build, confident swagger. He was with a smaller companion, also hooded and carrying a backpack, and they looked around pensively as their swiped card was accepted at the service entrance.

He called over PC Wishaw and pointed to the screen. "He's definitely one of them! Alert security! Clear the building! They're inside!"

The petite PC smashed her hand on a big, red plastic button, setting off a loud alarm, as she dashed across the room to call her superior. "Code red alert! Clear the building and get armed officers and bomb disposal to the service area! There are two of them and they're carrying a backpack!"

Ken appeared at the door and waved at George to follow him. With all the commotion no one paid them much attention and Ken guided them down a circular stone stairway into the bowels of the ancient building. "Stevo's savvy enough to avoid CCTV cameras. Guy Fawkes identified the most vulnerable spot, and my hunch is that they'll go for historical irony and head for the basement. The original cellars are no longer there, but there are store rooms under the building."

George's heart was beating fast as an adrenalin rush hit him. He had promised Sunny that he would remain in the control room and not get dragged into anything dangerous. Now he was scampering after Ken along low-ceilinged dimly-lit tunnels, running his fingers along the cold, clammy stone walls and wondering if they were below the level of the river. Ken stopped abruptly and held a finger up to his lips. He peered around a corner, and soon George could hear the sound of muffled voices and objects being dragged across the concrete floor.

"It's them!" Ken whispered urgently. "They're planting high explosives; we don't have much time. Come on!" Before George had time to think, Ken rushed around the corner and dived on the back of the bigger of the two hunched hooded figures. Stevo's surprised face looked up as Ken wrestled him to the ground. George was left facing off with a very aggressive-looking woman he recognised from the photo in Ken's folder – Dervla. She screamed with rage and rushed at George, kicking his knee and causing him to fall, and punching him in the face on his way down. With no self-defense skills, he was no match for her, and could barely manage to shield his face from her blows.

Before long, the younger, fitter and stronger terrorists had overpowered both Ken and George, who were expertly gagged and bound together with duct tape. A gloating Dervla said, "Dad's Army is no match for us! Just sit there quietly and watch us set these bomb timers. In five minutes from now the British Parliament will be a pile of rubble strewn with the dismembered limbs of fascists, and you've got ringside seats."

Within two minutes their work was done. Stevo and Dervla waved a patronising 'bye bye' to the two bound men as they ran down a dark tunnel, no doubt having planned their escape route. Ken struggled furiously and tried to roll over. George followed his lead and they rolled towards an exposed pipe bracket where Ken rubbed his taped hands until they snapped free. Ripping the duct tape off both of them, he sprang towards the timing device and shouted, "George, you get out, and point bomb disposal in this direction. I'll try to disarm the timer!"

George limped as fast as he could along a whitewashed tunnel, passing armed officers whom he directed towards Ken's location. A chink of sunlight appeared in front of him and he reached for the emergency door release just as the almighty BOOM of an explosion behind him pushed him bodily out of the door, cartwheeling through the air over a neatly-mown patch of lawn. It was the second time in barely three weeks.

"Oh no... Not again..." he moaned, then darkness.

My mind hummed on neutral as I surveyed the sombre faces in the courtroom, not hearing the repeated question of the solicitor. All eyes were fixed on me, waiting for the next words to tumble out of my mouth. Yes, technically speaking, I was responsible. In as much as I was the duty manager at the time of the accident. Funny word, 'accident'. A random happening. A chance event, as if the gods had mischievously intervened in the affairs of mere mortals. But a baby died and blame has to be apportioned, or absolved. I read the prepared statement, the one given to me by the company lawyers. Then the judge will decide where the heavy burden of blame lies, if anywhere. There are other runners in this race. The young sister, left to mind the baby. The mother, who went to buy cigarettes. It's out of my hands, entwined in legalese and the cold weave of fate...

"Mister Osborne, how are you feeling?" a nurse said, slowly coming into focus as she leaned over him. George groaned and turned away, falling into a fretful sleep.

GEORGE PEERED AT the TV on the hospital room wall through tired and blurred eyes. His head pounded and his ears were ringing as he tried to focus. He was in a mini-ward with three others, all survivors from the Westminster bombing, as a news reporter described it.

"You can see the thick pall of smoke behind me still rising from the river side of the Houses of Parliament. The structure withstood the blast and is still intact. We now know that brave security officers prevented a large device from detonating, however a secondary device, possibly a booby trap bomb, did explode, causing minor damage and injuries to a number of security personnel. More on this later as the story unfolds, but for now, the security forces are saying that the terror group, the Anti-Poverty League, have claimed responsibility for the largely unsuccessful attempt to destroy the Houses of Parliament. Back to the studio…"

George turned to his heavily-bandaged neighbour and said, "I guess we're lucky to be alive. Have you heard any news on my friend, Ken? He's the one who was defusing the bomb." The man turned awkwardly towards him and slurred a thick, dry response, "No mate, I've just come to. I was caught in the corridor, behind you. Our anti-blast suits and helmets took the force of the explosion; otherwise it would have been worse. I hope they catch the bastards who did this."

George lapsed into silent reflection. How many were injured? Had anyone died? What had happened to Ken? Was he alive or dead? A vision of the face of his friend, Dave, floated before him, laughing just before the blast that killed him. Now his friend and ally, Ken, might also be one of their victims. If so, he would no doubt get a posthumous medal for bravery, after George told them of his attempts to defuse the timer on the bomb, but that would be small comfort to his friends and family.

He turned his attention back to the news. A state of emergency had been declared, and armed soldiers and police had set up roadblocks everywhere. No arrests had been made, and there was much speculation about the Anti-Poverty League in the media. They had certainly upped their profile and got people terrified and talking about them.

Inspector Wilson appeared silently at his bedside, like an apparition from a horror film. His mournful expression was reminiscent of a basset hound, "How are you feeling today?" It was a rhetorical question. His head was buried in his notebook. "We've had a lead on Dervla and Tommy, and we're hopeful of finding them soon. It's a terrible business alright. I've brought someone to visit you. She's now under police protection, but she may as well be in London as anywhere."

George managed a cracked smile as Sunny came into the room and kissed him gently on the forehead. "George, I'm so glad you survived! It's all so awful; and poor Ken..." She sat on the chair and said what was really on her mind. "George, you could have been killed! What were you thinking going after such dangerous terrorists? It's all so terrible, like a nightmare that never ends..." "There, there." George reached over and patted her leg. "What happened to Ken? No one here has told me anything."

Wilson and Sunny exchanged looks, and the Inspector took it on himself to break the news. "Ken Jones is alive but in intensive care. He sustained massive injuries during the explosion of what we believe was a small booby trap device. His body suit took much of the shrapnel impact and saved him. Fortunately for us, he had disconnected the timer from the high explosives so the main bomb didn't go off. He's a very brave man. We all hope he pulls through."

George sat back and took it in. He'd been at the scene of two bombings by the Anti-Poverty League and had survived them both. His companions had not been so lucky. Poor Dave had died and now Ken was fighting for his life. Looking at Wilson, he asked, "Any developments on finding them?"

"They made a clean getaway during the confusion. But like I said before, we have some ideas on where they might have gone. I guess our security measures are not as good as they should be. But you're both well out of it. We've detailed a female police officer to shadow Sunny as a precaution, but I doubt they will spend any time coming after you two. You can forget this romantic *Famous Four* or whatever you call yourselves. It's over for the three of you."

George managed a doleful response, "Actually, it was *The Thames Valley Defence Force*, and we are happy to disband. Poor old Ken. At least he's prevented them trying to re-write history with a successful Gunpowder Plot. You've got to give us some credit, though. Through our surveillance and intelligence gathering on the group it has helped reduced their impact and given you more to go on."

Wilson replied tetchily, "Yes, you did your bit, and will get thanks in due course. But now focus on rest and recovery. We'll wrap this up soon, believe me." With that, he smiled and nodded to Sunny and departed.

She managed a tearful smile and said, "The Thames Valley Two – battered, bruised and hiding in fear from terrorists who are still out there and planning more murder and madness." They both looked up at the TV pictures of the smoking building, surrounded by fire engines and police cars.

The man in the next bed turned up the volume as a statement was about to be read out. A grey-haired man wearing a dark suit and standing in front of Buckingham Palace prepared to read from a sheet of paper.

"His Majesty, King Charles III, wishes to reassure the country that he is in the process of establishing a new Privy Council to govern the country and consult on a way forward. He unreservedly condemns all acts of violence and has instructed the civil, armed and security forces to remain on high alert. He expresses his deep abhorrence at the attempt to destroy the Houses of Parliament building and congratulates the security officers who were able to curtail the impact of the atrocity. He calls for calm and assures you all that the matter of governing the country is in hand, and the defense of the realm from anarchists and terrorist groups is under control.

"The identity of the members of the Privy Council will remain confidential until all security threats have been neutralised. In the meantime, a state of emergency continues, and all must observe a ten-hour curfew, from nine o'clock in the evening until seven o'clock the following morning. Retail and other businesses will adjust their opening time accordingly. His Majesty implores you all to remain calm, as these measures are temporary and are necessary until the security situation normalises."

A brief pause, momentary eye contact with camera, a slight cough, and then he continued. "You are advised to remain in your homes unless you have a good reason to be out, and are required to carry a photo ID to produce on request. Your patience and co-operation is requested when stopped by armed patrols and at road blocks where random vehicle searches will be conducted. Appearing on the screen is a telephone number you can call should you observe any suspicious behaviour in your area or know of anyone answering the description of the terrorists described after this message. We apologise for the suspension of the internet and limited telephone connection. God save the king!"

George turned to a startled-looking Sunny and said, "Wow! That'll be a bombshell to most of the country. So now it begins. Indefinite suspension of all civil liberties, rights of movement and access to means of communication. It's almost as if the Establishment has been waiting for something like this to seize control of the nation. Who's really in charge? George Orwell would laugh if he were alive to see this. *Nineteen Eighty-Four* should be re-issued under the title, *Twenty Twenty-Six*...he was only 42 years out with his prediction."

"Eric Blair," said the man in the next bed.

"Eh?" replied George.

"Eric Blair was George Orwell's real name He worked in intelligence during the second world war, and formed his ideas of a one-party totalitarian state in a pub not far from here. Next they'll be telling us who the new 'Big Brother' is. My guess is the aging monarch's hand is being guided by the head of MI5."

Sunny tried to distract him by swinging the conversation to family matters. This brought some relief to both of them, and not for the first time, George felt glad to be alive. But once the chit-chat petered out, he lapsed back into a sullen silence. He felt utterly helpless, like a leaf being blown about on the wind – the secretive Privy Council had control of the country and their lives. Hard-won personal freedoms, fought for over hundreds of years, had now been suspended by Royal Decree. Law and order was breaking down as rioters and looters took control of towns and cities. They now faced a very uncertain future.

George dragged himself out of his stupor and whispered to Sunny, "I'm reminded of that scene in *Casablanca* when Humphrey Bogart turns to Ingrid Bergman and says something like, 'We had to pick the end of the world to fall in love'". They smiled at each other and held hands, brown-eyed girl to blue-eyed boy, as if no one else existed. Well, for a short while. Then George asked her, "By the way, where's Derrick?"

CHAPTER NINE

A KNIFE OF yellow light probed the alleyway where Derrick and his mate, Vapes, hid behind a wheelie bin. They had scarpered during the confusion outside the Mega Mini Mart after riot police arrived and chased them and other looters. They had taken their coloured pills and, on a hyperactive rush, had looted and set fire to the building. Derrick had acted as part of the gang, participating in a manic trolley dash, as frightened staff and shoppers ran from the store, before Charly and a few others poured paraffin over the place and set it ablaze.

Chaos reigned on the streets of Slough, with genuine protestors standing their ground and gang members scurrying for cover. Derrick, starting to come down from his amphetamine high, ducked into a dark alley behind the shops. Now the police were clearing the area and searching for stragglers, scooping up struggling strays and putting them into the back of black-windowed vans. They were no doubt looking for anyone they could charge with criminal damage.

"Keep low and follow me," Derrick whispered as he moved in a crouched run further down the alley, away from the flashlights and high-vis jackets. At the end of the alley there was a chain mesh fence, with a hole at the bottom corner through which animals must have passed.

"I'm not a cat, man!" Vapes whined, as Derrick tried to enlarge the opening by pulling on the wire mesh. The police were getting closer, and this seemed their only chance of escape.

"Del!" Vapes hoarsely whispered, "Have you seen this?" He pointed to a yellow warning sign on the fence, with a red bolt of lightning flashed across and bold letters: 'Power Substation Keep Out'.

Derrick nodded and crawled through the opening. "It's this way or be arrested by the cops." Vapes squeezed through after him, and they tried to push down the wire mesh behind them, before making a careful crouched walk across the desolate and rubbish-strewn patch of land. The moon was rising and gave just enough light to make out the shape of a small brick building and the electricity conductor rods rising from the ground like Doctor Who monsters that buzzed a warning in an alien language.

ESSIE WAITED IN nervous excitement at arrivals in Heathrow Terminal Five. Dex had just texted her, saying he was in the baggage hall. She was dolled up to make a good impression and barely admitted to herself that she had fallen in love with this big, brash, rich American. She was in the middle of end of year exams, and would have to manage her time with Dex. They were coming through now, and she craned her neck to try and pick him out of a huddle of weary travellers dragging wheeled cases behind them.

"Dex!" she yelled, when he came into view. His face lit up in a wide smile and they collided into the intimate embrace of lovers meeting after separation. She threw her arms around his neck, pulling him down towards her as she kissed him passionately. Opening her eyes, she recoiled in alarm at the grinning face of his father's security guard, Mac, standing behind him.

"Oh my God! You've brought your security guy! Why?" she asked.

"Well hello to you too, honey, give me a chance to catch my breath!" Dex stepped back and held her by the shoulders, his eyes full of admiration. She looked at him and then at Mac.

"Yeah, my Dad's got some business matters on the go in London, so he sent Mac over to deal with them. Don't worry; he won't be following us around! I'm all yours for two weeks, and then I must get back to Harvard for my end of semester assessment. Although, as you know I'm on a sporting scholarship, so it won't be too rough!"

He took her by her arm and led her away. She was still glancing suspiciously behind at Mac, who fell into step about five metres behind Dex, head scanning suspiciously from side to side. A uniformed rock choir added to the noise in the huge domed hall, singing a harmonic version of 'Somebody to Love' to welcome new arrivals. A man shaking a collection tin smiled warmly and randomly asked passers-by where there had come from. He eyed Mac but, seeing his steely unfriendly glare, quickly moved his gaze on to Essie.

"Welcome to London! Where are you from, young lady?"

It was not his lucky day, as she gave him a curt, "I'm a Londoner, mister! Just because I'm mixed race doesn't mean you can assume I'm foreign! As it happens, the white guy is a Yank. Ask him!" She threw her head back and walked off, adopting a haughty manner. Dex smiled apologetically at the well-meaning collector and produced a handful of US coins from his pocket which he quickly pushed into the tin, whilst mouthing, "sorry," as he hurried after her.

"Let's get a cab," he said, taking charge. "I don't wanna battle through crowds on your subway."

"It's the Underground," she corrected. She poked her tongue at him.

He grinned like a schoolboy, "Give me a minute with Mac, will ya?"

She kept their place on the taxi rank, whilst the two men talked off to one side. After a minute they shook hands and Mac headed for the Underground.

"Don't worry, honey, he'll be staying someplace else and going about my Dad's business. Did I say how beautiful you look?" They managed an awkward hug before bundling themselves into a black taxi. "Gee, I love your London cabs! Really quaint. The Ritz, please!"

They checked into a lovely suite, overlooking Green Park, and tried out the king-sized bed. Words were not needed: eye contact and lustful smirks were enough. They threw their clothes off and climbed into opposite sides of the huge bed, jiggling a bit until they met in the middle. It was still early stages in their relationship, so more physical bonding was urgently required. Limbs entwined, they got down to it. The perfect way to kill an hour on a grey overcast London afternoon.

THEY PICKED THEIR way past broken glass and bits of wood that had been thrown into the rectangular fenced-off compound, turning it into a dangerous rubbish tip by the willfully ignorant, the casually lawless and local rebellious youths. A doll's dead eyes reflected in the pale moonlight to increase their sense of alarm as they paused to listen to the police officers checking the fence at the end of the alleyway. Torch beams swept the power station grounds as they stood with their backs to the small building in the centre. Derrick was frantic with worry about being questioned by the police and linked to the mini-mart looting and burning incident. They must get away.

"Don't move!" Derrick whispered to his terrified companion. Vapes, so named because of his love of smoking e-cigarettes, was of a nervous disposition. He kept a low profile in the gang and was easily swayed and manipulated by the bully-girl Charly. If she needed support for any of her wild ideas, she would turn to Vapes first for assent, confident that the others would then fall into line.

"I'm scared, Del. What if they catch us? My Dad'll kill me!" he whined.

"Shhh!" Derrick hissed, as a beam or torchlight swept past their feet.

"Who's there?" shouted a male policeman with a booming voice that shattered the quiet night.

Derrick put his hand across his quivering friend's chest, but it was not enough to stop him from breaking cover and running away from the voice of authority and the yellow searching beam. Derrick stayed where he was and watched in dismay as Vapes's foot crunched a glass bottle and he swayed to his left, like a drunken sailor on shore leave.

"Oy! You! Stop!" the policeman shouted.

Vapes half-turned towards the copper and lost balance, instinctively reaching out with his left hand to find something to break his fall. He did find something. An electric conductor, sitting in the dark like an anorexic Dalek, humming quietly, waiting for.... Flash! Zap! Vapes' dancing body lit up the night sky as 10,000 volts of electricity surged through him. Derrick could do nothing but watch as his friend jerked, sizzled and jolted, a look of horror mixed with surprise on his face, his hair standing on end. He collapsed to the ground after what seemed an age, but was probably no more than 10 seconds.

Derrick, shocked at the sight, edged along the wall, thinking there was nothing he could do to help and knowing that he should not touch his friend's charged body. He rounded the corner of the building and picked his way to the far end of the compound, climbing up onto a brick wall that bordered someone's backyard. Behind him he heard the police officers reach the body and call for an ambulance on their radio. He lay on top of the wall, hidden by darkness, and looked back at the smoking remains of his friend. An awful thought came to him, but he couldn't un-think it. Vapes had been vaporised. It was a sad, gruesome, and ultimately ironic ending; a victim of his own fearful nature. He died lit up like lights on a Christmas tree - an image that would forever be ingrained in Derek's memory.

Derrick dropped down into a gloomy paved backyard and sobbed silently as he stood with his back to the wall for a few minutes, gathering his thoughts, recovering his breath, and listening to the police dealing with yet another tragic accident. When his eyes adjusted to the gloom he saw that the wall to his right had a wooden door that must go onto an alleyway. He carefully pulled back a bolt and opened the door, just as the kitchen light came on in the house. He slipped out, shutting the door behind him, and ran for his life along the alley between the backs of two rows of terraced houses. Out into the street, he walked home, avoiding main roads and patrolling police vans.

FOR DEX THIS was normal, but for Essie it was a rare treat – dipping into the world of the super-rich, and somehow managing to act like she belonged there. It was easier in New York, which to her had been a faraway fairy tale adventure. This was London, and although she had walked past the Ritz Hotel on Piccadilly many times, this was the first time she had been inside. It wasn't just any room either, they were in a magnificent suite on the west side, overlooking the park. Famous people must have slept in that bed – royalty, film stars, oil sheiks and villains. This was most definitely the world of the extremely wealthy, a world in which Dex looked supremely at ease. Despite their cultural differences, she felt comfortable with Dex. She was hooked on his casual charm, good looks and easy, satisfying love-making. She finished applying her make-up and went down to breakfast.

Dex ordered kippers, a quaint English culinary thing he loved, and she followed suit. He read the *New York Times* and she scanned *The Times*. 'State of Emergency Declared' shouted the headline. She turned to the fashion section.

"Have you noticed that our Times is *The Times*, whilst yours is a copied version? Just like our golf tournament is The Open, and yours is the US Open? Britain invents and gives to the world. Don't forget that you're a colonial visiting your mother country!"

Dex laughed loudly, startling other guests. "Yeah! I'm just an old country hick coming in from the village! The only difference is, I own the village, and your old mother is a poor widow in debt to me and us good ol' colonial folks!" They chuckled as they feasted on the perfect breakfast.

"Seen this?" she showed him the front page story. "My dad's a hero, you know. He was one of the group, described here as The Thames Valley Defence Force, who tried to stop the terrorist bomb from going off. They succeeded in stopping the main bomb that would have brought down the Houses of Parliament, but a booby trap device exploded, injuring him and badly injuring his friend who took the full force of the blast."

Dex put down his paper and sat up, fully alert. "Wow! That's amazing! Your dad's involved in battling terrorists? I didn't realise your family was involved. Let me see that paper."

She handed it over and pointed out the bit that mentioned George. This was a bit of luck for Dex, who was in reality a covert spy for the CIA, posing as an exchange student. His uncle had recruited him into the 'family business,' and he had taken a year out for training before going to Harvard as part of his cover. They had asked him to find out what he could about who was behind the Anti-Poverty League and how they operated, so they could do a terrorist risk assessment for the USA.

"That's so cool," he said after a few minutes, "your dad's a real hero; I'd love to meet him."

"Yeah, I'm sure that would be fine. He's being discharged from hospital today and I'm due to call him later and pop over there to see him. I'll let you know if he's up for receiving visitors," she said breezily. "How's your schedule?"

"Well, honey, I'm gonna have to leave you for the rest of the morning to attend to some family business. Let's meet back here for lunch at one. The rest of my day's free - we can do whatever you want. You organise it."

"That's okay, I'll head back to my digs for a few hours, and then call my dad. I'll let you know what he says when we meet at lunch." They kissed and she headed for Green Park tube station, feeling warm and happy and barely noticing the armed police officers watchfully scanning the crowd. *My dad's a real live hero*, she thought as she skipped down the stairs, *much more than just plain George the retired railway man*.

GEORGE WAS POTTERING around his flat, making a stiff, half-hearted effort to tidy up after Sunny left him to attend to her own flat and family, and was glad of the interruption when his mobile phone started playing a weedy version of *Tubular Bells*.

"Oh hi, love. Nice to hear from you," he said brightly at hearing his daughter's voice. "Yes, I've been released from hospital; only minor cuts and bruising. I feel a bit sore, but otherwise not too bad. Poor old Ken is still in intensive care with tubes coming out of his arms and up his nose. I saw him before I left. He's still unconscious but stable, poor chap. Anyway, are you coming over to see me?"

"Oh yes, Dad. Remember I told you about Dex? Well he's in London as part of the student exchange programme, and he read about your heroic exploits in the paper and wants to meet you," she chattered excitedly. "How about we come over this evening? Perhaps we could go out for a pub meal? Dex would love that."

"Great idea! I've no inclination to cook. And you could both meet my new, erm, girlfriend - my neighbour, Sunny."

"Wow, Dad! Didn't know you had a new lady friend! Good for you. You've been alone too long. I can't wait to meet her. Let's say we'll be at yours for seven. And don't forget to invite Del. Haven't seen him since the last time you were in hospital! Oh, and by the way, I told Dex that you're a transport consultant, so if you wouldn't mind..."

"What did you say that for?"

"Well, his family and friends are all well-off and have important-sounding jobs. Sorry Dad, I just felt drawn into a game of...I just wanted to impress them and make out I was..."

George got it, "You wanted them to think you're a posh girl from a posh family, eh? There was a silent pause and George continued, "OK I understand, love, I'll be a transport consultant for the evening. It's alright, I'm kind of pleased that you're mixing with the rich and influential, but you don't need to be ashamed of where you're from. We're all decent hard-working people. Remember that. Also, it's best he doesn't come here, to the estate; we should meet in a posh pub – I'll let you know where."

"I'm sorry, Dad. I didn't mean to put you down or anything..." She had a slightly upset tone in her voice.

"It's alright, love. Not a problem. I'll text you the details when I've booked a table. I'll see you both later."

"Thanks, Dad. You're the best! See you later, love you."

She rang off and George was left grinning at the slim plastic device in his hand. 'Must go over and tell Sunny,' he thought. 'No, smarten myself up first. After all, I'm a Transport Consultant.'

George went to Derrick's closed bedroom door and knocked on it.

"Del? Are you awake, Son?"

There was a moment's silence followed by a shuffling of bed clothes. "Dad, I'm not feeling well, leave me alone," he mumbled. It was the morning after his daring escape from the police, who had been searching for and scooping up rioters and looters who had completely trashed Slough town centre in an orgy of destruction. His friend, Vapes, had died horribly in front of him, twisting manically in an electric dance of death. The image would not go away, despite shaking his head and rubbing his eyes.

"Alright, I'll get up," he croaked as he sat up and surveyed his untidy room. Last night's clothes lay on the floor, a pair of pants on his computer keyboard. Rhianna's sexy smirk had become a mocking taunt. He knew he had to avoid the Run Posse from now on. The police would be looking for those involved in looting and burning down the mini-mart. How could he have got involved? His head ached and his mouth was dry as he suffered the after effects of the amphetamine pills he had taken. No more drugs. He resolved to follow his father's advice and pass his driving test to help him find a job. No more time-wasting, the future beckons. He got showered and shaved off his gang-identifier neckbeard, admiring his clean-shaven image in the mirror.

George noticed the clean-cut improvement to his sheepish son's appearance and resisted the temptation to make fun of him. Maybe it was a sign of a new serious approach, which should be encouraged.

"I'm making us a cooked brunch, Son. The works, with a nice mug of tea. Come and sit down. Your sister and her new fella are coming over later, and we're going out to a posh pub – the Belvedere Arms near Windsor Great Park - for dinner, so no disappearing."

He was busy frying, toasting and pouring boiling water. "After we've eaten I want you to come with Sunny, Ravi and myself for a big shopping trip. We may have to go further afield, to the big ASDA near the motorway, as the state of emergency has got people panicking. Our nearest supermarkets have been burnt and looted. Also, the nine o'clock curfew starts tonight, so we'll see armed soldiers manning roadblocks. The terrorists are winning and the new government are under pressure to get to grips with a country sliding into chaos. Things are going to get more difficult, that's for sure. Come on, eat up." Derrick was happy for the distraction. Anything to keep his mind off the events of the previous night.

ESSIE INSISTED ON a walk to Piccadilly Circus, to show Dex the statue of Eros.

"Eros was the winged Greek god of love, who fell in love with a beautiful mortal woman called Psyche," Essie explained to Dex, fluttering her eyelashes at him coquettishly. A cavalcade of street performers and artists crowded around the famous fountain, over which the statue of a posing Eros aimed his arrow. "Whoever he fires his arrow at falls in love with him. This was how he ensnared Psyche and made her his lover." She pulled his arm to guide him away from a group of jugglers. "Watch your wallet around here," she advised.

"Why? There are cops everywhere!" he laughed.

They wandered back to their hotel, arm in arm, past hundreds of shoppers and tourists hurrying about their business in this permanently busy stretch of London. As Dex was showering, she made another call to her dad, just to make sure he wasn't upset and was fully onboard with the evening's arrangements. He was in a chipper mood and told her that it would be just him and a suitably briefed Derrick, as Sunny had declined the invitation on the grounds that it was an Osborne family occasion. She came off her mobile thinking how complicated things became once little white lies were thrown into the mix. Dex knew they weren't a wealthy family, but she felt obliged to build and maintain a social facade to show they were *Middle Class Achievers*, as opposed to *Working Class Strugglers*. It wasn't just the British who were obsessed with class and status.

They arrived at 7pm sharp at the Belvedere Arms in Sunningdale, barely an hour's drive from their hotel. The uniformed chauffeur opened her door and Dex told him to pick them up in an hour. They were all conscious of the curfew and wanted to be back at the Ritz by then. The interior was a mock old English beamed coaching inn, and Dex smiled warmly and bowed slightly at the welcoming staff and a few startled customers. They looked like a Hollywood couple who had somehow got lost. They found George and Derrick waiting at their table. Both stood up for the formal greetings, and George had perhaps overdone it slightly by wearing a jacket and tie. Essie was pleased to see her twin looking well and smartly dressed.

"Del! Glad to see you've shaved off that scraggy beard!" she laughed.

"Wow! This sure is quaint!" said Dex, ducking to avoid the low beams.

They ordered drinks and Dex eye-balled George, "Mister Osborne, it's a pleasure to meet you. Your lovely daughter tells me that you're a transport consultant. That sounds interesting."

"Quite," said George, fiddling with his napkin. "I retired from the Railway Board and set up my own business, advising on transport policy and expansion," he lied, in a carefully rehearsed speech. He knew enough about the workings of the railways network and integrated transportation systems to be able to blag on the subject with ease. He was happy to do it for the sake of his lovely, intelligent daughter, whose life choices had so far been pretty well made. He instantly warmed to Dex, as almost everyone did, and could see why she would be attracted to this handsome, cultured and charming young man.

"Tell me a bit about your family, Dexter?" he said, sipping on a gin and tonic.

"Well, Mister Osborne, the Poindexter family is one of the leading East Coast families, descended from the Founding Fathers who came from England in the 17th century. Members of my family have served in the armed forces, in politics and in the security service. I'm currently studying history at Harvard, although I have to confess I'm only there on a sports scholarship and I have to row hard in their eights team to justify my place." He winked at Derrick, making a rowing motion with his arms.

George smiled warmly and said, "You're most welcome to our humble corner of England, and I'm pleased to see my daughter looking so happy and relaxed. I just hope you both devote the appropriate amount of time to studying and come away with university degrees at the end of it!"

They ordered from the dinner menu – both George and Dex were attracted to the lavish specification of the Casterbridge nine ounce 28-day aged rib-eye steak. Derrick ordered the steak, Doombar ale and mushroom pie, and Essie fancied trying the sticky crispy duck salad. Whilst waiting for their food, Essie gave the censored version of her week at Harvard and romantic long weekend in New York. Soon the food arrived and Dex tucked into his steak like a starving man. Essie caught up on family news as they ate, pumping George for information on his new girlfriend, Sunny. Whilst waiting for dessert, Dex excused himself to go outside to smoke a cigar, and asked George to join him. They stood facing the ancient forest of Windsor in the rear garden, and George accepted a thin Cuban cigar, although he had not smoked for many years.

"Sir," Dex began, "I heard from Essie that you were recently injured helping the security services prevent a bomb going off in your Houses of Parliament building. That sounds amazing, and very brave, if you don't mind me saying."

George grinned like a boy who had won a prize. "Yes, it was pretty hairy at the time. I had got involved with a vigilante group who helped the police identify a gang of terrorists calling themselves the Anti-Poverty League. As we had some contact with the terrorists, including making an attempt to infiltrate their group and then rescue one of our members who they were holding prisoner, the cops asked myself and a colleague to sit in their control room and try to identify them if they approached the Houses of Parliament building, otherwise known as the Palace of Westminster."

"Wow, Sir! That's fascinating! To think you're a regular James Bond type of guy! This stuff could be in a movie!"

George warmed to the subject, "Well, my friend Ken and I tracked down the bombers to a storeroom under the building where Guy Fawkes had been a few hundred years earlier in the original gunpowder plot. We fought them but were overpowered and tied up, but managed to free ourselves. Sadly, we only partly succeeded and my friend, Ken, managed to diffuse the main bomb, but was seriously injured when a secondary device exploded. I was only slightly injured in the blast. Unfortunately, they got away, and are still at large. Talking about it now, it's incredible to think this all happened just a few days ago."

The conversation was heading in the right direction for Dex. "You're very brave, Mister Osborne, and a national hero. I'm sure they'll give you a medal and you'll get to meet the king! By the way, you said you knew the identity of the terrorists. Do you know their names?"

George eyed him and drew on his cigar, trying not to choke. "Well, Dexter, the police have asked me not to discuss the details with anyone not connected with the case, so I'm not sure I should name names..."

Dex held up his hands in a backing-off gesture. "Hey, I fully understand, Mister Osborne. National security and all that. Hell, I should know better, my uncle is high up in US national security. But here's the thing. If you tell me those names, then maybe I could get my uncle to run a security check on them to see if they are known to our guys and if so I could give you feedback which you could pass on."

"Dexter, I've told the cops I'm well out of it now, and I'm sure our people are already talking to your people. I'd prefer to stay out of it. My friend Ken is still in intensive care and may not pull through..."

"Gee, I'm sorry Mister Osborne. Of course I'll drop it. Just wanted to help, that's all. They seem like determined terrorists who will most likely strike again if they're not taken out." He could see George was not for budging and they went back inside. As George went to the men's room, Dex whispered something in Essie's ear.

After dessert, Essie and Dex checked the time and made to leave. George insisted on paying, waving away Dex's offer to cover the bill. As they made their way to the door, Essie took her dad by the arm and put her head on his shoulder.

"Dad, I'm so happy to see you alive and well after that horrendous bombing incident. I'd really like to meet Sunny, and get to know her. How about I pop over tomorrow? Dex has some private matters to attend to, so I've got some free time. Could you ask her if she'll be available for tea tomorrow afternoon?"

"Of course, darling." George embraced and kissed her warmly. "Just call me before you start off. Dexter, it's been great meeting you, and please look after my daughter. She's my little treasure!"

On the drive back they couldn't help but notice army trucks and police vans everywhere, setting up roadblocks at major road junctions as they left Sunningdale, in readiness for the curfew. Dex turned to Essie and said, "Sorry to have to ask you darling, but we can really help your security people out if we know the names of these terrorists. I'm sure you can get the names from Sunny, as she'll most likely not see it as a matter of secrecy. But be sure to talk to her alone, away from your dad. Did I say how beautiful you look tonight? I love you." The deal was sealed with a kiss. He needed those names.

CHAPTER TEN

FEAR AND UNCERTAINTY had gripped the country following the declaration of a state of emergency by the interim government, quickly followed by the nine o'clock curfew, with armed police and soldiers manning roadblocks at main road junctions. In fact, the roadblocks had remained in place the following day, and drivers were being randomly stopped and asked where they were going and if deemed to be suspicious, pulled to the side of the road and their vehicle searched. For those old enough to remember the Troubles in Northern Ireland during the 1970s, it was a familiar scene.

Tougher policing from uncompromising franchise security firms led to an emptying of the streets and a decrease in rioting and looting, but hospitals were filling up with the injured as less care was taken when dealing with protesters. Battle lines had been drawn, and as a result, most people stayed at home, only going out for emergency supplies. With few people going to work, speculation was rife in the media about an imminent collapse of the economy. City of London bankers and investment sharks were already swimming off to warmer waters, mainly to European or North American cities.

The effects of free market capitalism had rendered the UK a tame, toothless and passive country of non-producing consumers. Now a non-EU member, the fragile economy was barely kept afloat by the proceeds of financial investments, and with the financial sector jumping ship, there was a growing sense of isolation and impending doom. There was opportunity in weakness, and opposition groups were becoming increasingly militant and pro-Republican, with many seeing a revolution as the only way to sweep aside the ruling elite, now in power after defenestrating democracy. After all, it was the Lord Chief

Justice who had declared a constitutional crisis and called on the head of state, King Charles III, to form a 'temporary' government. There had been no referendum.

Dex woke up early and kissed a just-waking Essie on the cheek. "Gotta run, honey. Emergency meeting of my dad's company executives over this crisis. Call you later." With that he was off, and she was left to her own devices for the morning. She showered and called George over breakfast.

"Hi Dad, yeah it was a lovely evening. We both really enjoyed it. Yes, Dex was suitably impressed with you and Del. He's like a boy, fascinated by spies and James Bond. He kept talking about it on the way home. I've got free time today. Yes, I'll do some revision this morning. He's gone off to a meeting. Yes, I can come over at about 12. See you then." She went to the nearby Selfridges department store on Oxford Street and bought some clothes, using Dex's credit card. Make hay while the sun shines, she thought gaily as she enjoyed the luxury of not worrying about cost.

George welcomed his daughter warmly, admiring her designer clothes, and introduced her to the waiting Sunny in his living room. If Essie was unprepared to meet an Indian lady, she didn't show it. The strong aroma of Dior perfume filled the room as she embraced her father's new girlfriend and they fell into friendly chat before their bums hit the seats. They drank tea and shared their edited life stories, as George fidgeted and fussed. Essie needed to get some one-on-one time with Sunny and asked her father for something she knew he wouldn't have.

"I'll just pop down to the shop, that's if they're still open, and get some Hobnobs and cakes."

With that he was off and they were alone.

Essie eased into the topic in mind, "I bet you were scared being held prisoner by those terrorists. What was it like?"

110

Sunny stirred her tea, "Well it was truly terrifying. There were two of them interrogating both of us, and then Stevo got up and joined them, saying that he had been on their side all along, and I was now their captive! I was shocked, and they tied me up, quite roughly. Look, you can still see the rope marks." She showed Essie some bruising on her wrists and ankles.

"Wow, that sounds frightening! You poor thing!" Essie said. "Then you were dramatically rescued by my Dad and Ken?"

"Oh yes! I was locked in a bedroom when Ken tapped on the window. I was so happy and relieved to see his face! He was on a ladder and between us we were able to get the window open for me to escape. George was holding the bottom of the ladder, and we hardly had time to hug as the alarm was ringing and Ken made us run across the lawn and to his car. It was just like the movies, I tell you!"

They laughed and then Essie innocently asked, "So Stevo was your friend up to that point, wasn't he an army mate of Ken's?"

"Yes he was. Ken was very angry at his act of betrayal."

"Was Stevo his real name?"

"That's how we were introduced to him."

"Okay, and you knew the others in the terrorist group because you met them at a party. Is that right?"

"Yes, I went with Stevo to infiltrate their group. Stevo met one of his army friends there, Tommy Styles, he was called. His girlfriend, an Irish woman who was one of their leaders, tried to make friends with me. I didn't like her. She was very pushy and very confident. The third one was a man called Peter."

"Oh, I know what you mean. I've met some women like that. What did you say she was called?"

This was the big one. Sunny sipped her tea before answering.

"Well, I'm not really supposed to say. The police have insisted on secrecy and their names have been kept out of the media so far...but between you and me, she's called Dervla. More like Devil, if you ask me."

"A pushy Irish woman called Dervla. She sounds dangerous to me! You're very brave, and have a hell of a story to tell."

George banged the front door to announce his return. "Not a story we can tell right now," Sunny whispered. "Those terrorists are still out there, planning God-knows-what atrocity." She leaned back and smiled as George came in with biscuits and cakes. "Hello dear. What have you got for us?"

George set the items on the coffee table, pulled off his coat and hung it in the hall. "The corner shop is still open but is heavily guarded by a bunch of Indian youths with serious weapons. I managed to buy some biscuits, cakes, and some more bottled water to add to our stocks. Prices have doubled. This situation is getting out of hand. Lucky we stocked up yesterday."

Essie managed to get Del out of his room and away from his gaming for a few minutes to say goodbye. Her driver was waiting outside and she had to meet Dex for lunch. She had a few names to pass on to him, and they could no doubt find out the full identity of 'Stevo' from Ken Jones' and Tommy Styles' army records. As for the mysterious Dervla, well, she may already be known to the security services.

Sunny's eyes widened in terror and she pointed out of the window, shrinking back into the room and unable to speak. A mob had appeared and was surrounding Essie's chauffeur-driven car. Del recognised the tell-tale figure of Charly Smith and the rest of the Run Posse. Hoods up and carrying sticks and baseball bats, they were tapping on the driver's window, trying to persuade the undoubtedly terrified man to open his door.

"That's your mob, isn't it, Son?" George asked Derrick.

Del went pale and hung back. He had not talked about his ordeal, the looting and arson episode, or the death of his friend. "Dad, I'm trying to avoid them. I don't want to be in their gang anymore."

George saw that he was afraid and unwilling to be seen by them. He also wanted him to stay away from the street gang. "Alright. I've got some beer in the kitchen. Maybe I can convince them to get away from the car long enough for Essie to jump in and get back to her hotel. Quite frankly, love, you'll be safer there with Dex to watch out for you. Here, borrow my old raincoat to hide your posh clothes."

George insisted that just Essie and he go out, with a carrier bag of beer and snacks, and try for a quick getaway.

"Oy, what's going on here?" George put on his best act of bravado, standing tall and trying not to limp, like a cornered buffalo facing a pride of starving lions. Looking tough, but also with a non-threatening smile, he approached the group, some of whom he recognised as Del's former schoolmates. He made his way to Charly Smith, the big gang leader, and offered her the carrier bag.

"What's this, Mister Osborne, a bribe?" she said.

"Just being friendly, Charly. My daughter, Essie, you remember her? She needs to get back to town for a meeting. So if you don't mind..." He managed to prize a youth away from the rear door and the driver leaned over and released the door lock. Essie quickly got in and the engine started. She waved at George and he saw concern on her face as the car pulled away.

"Where's your Del, then?" Charly demanded.

"He's not here. He went to stay with my sister over in Bracknell. He's got a job interview," George casually lied, hoping they couldn't see anyone through the windows. She eyed him suspiciously, and looked past him to the flat.

"Oh, is that right, Mister Osborne?" she said menacingly. "Then you won't mind if I come in and have a look for him, will you? The cops are looking for him, due to the riots two days ago, and the fact that he was with one of our own who got killed. It's not just the cops who want to talk to him, I do as well." Some gang members sniggered at the mention of the riots, and Charly had a self-satisfied smirk on her face.

George didn't need to act surprised. He wasn't aware that the police were looking for him. They had not called at the flat. "Is that so? I never heard that. I haven't seen him for two days, as it happens." She stepped menacingly towards George. He backed away towards his gate and blocked her advance. "Look here, Charly. He's not around, and I'd rather not invite you lot in. Just take these beers and snacks as a goodwill gesture, for minding Essie's car. Job well done. I'll tell Del to come see you when he gets back."

He stared her down, and after a few seconds she stepped away and laughed. "Alright, Mister Osborne. Have it your way. But be sure to tell him I want to see him, and to tell the cops nuffink. We'll keep coming back here until he comes out. Thanks for the beers." With that they sauntered off, about fifteen strong, George calculated. A gang not to be crossed, he thought, as he returned to the safety of his flat.

"Here, Son, I want a word with you!" George said, as he locked the front door behind him.

MUNCHING BISCUITS, THEY sat in silence as pictures of roadblocks, military vehicles and riots dominated the news. A reporter warned of possible power cuts. Things were getting bad. George had only been out of hospital for a week and in that time the country had descended into lawless chaos. Previously friendly neighbourhood watch groups had armed themselves to protect their properties from roaming gangs who had grown in numbers and lost their fear of the law.

The television switched itself off and the table lamp went out. "Power cuts now. They're bound to target areas like this. We need to get out of here," Sunny said, jumping to her feet. "It's only a matter of time before the mob gets in or burns us out. Most of our neighbours have gone... the street is deserted, except for occasional gangs passing by. All we need now are zombies and we'll be in a scene from *28 Days Later!*" She hugged her daughter Dita and son Ravi.

George knew their situation was serious. The local gang was mainly white and they had been shouting racist threats as they moved through the estate. The multi-racial composition of the area would just add another layer of tension onto an already bad situation. Fear and insecurity would drive people into tribal groups. They knew that Del, their missing gang member, was of mixed race and that George was friendly with his Indian neighbours. They would be back.

George saw the concern and misery in their faces and said, "Yes, you're right. We've got to leave as soon as possible. I'll be Brendan Gleeson and you lot start packing. I'll sneak out and get the car ready. I've been doing a bit of contingency planning. I got a text a few days ago from a friend of mine who owns a guesthouse up in the Cotswolds. He says it's quiet there and we are welcome to stay. It's usually about two hours' drive, but with these roadblocks, who knows. Let's get moving."

"The Cotswolds?" Sunny grabbed his arm. "Isn't that where the rich people live, protected by private security check points and CCTV cameras?"

"Yes," George said, "we may be up against it to be admitted to the wealthy heart of England."

"Just as well as I have a spare Woolf's Head Security shirt and cap," Sunny grinned triumphantly. "And I'll be holding a tablet with their letterhead on a memo saying I'm conducting a review of security arrangements. That should do it."

They decided to leave immediately – it was early afternoon and they didn't want another sleepless night barricaded in the flat. George restricted each of them to one bag of clothing and personal effects. Food and drink were packed into boxes, and he found space for his new camping and birdwatching gear. Outside, George sniffed the air. A blackbird's song brought it home to him that there were no other sounds – no vehicles or flights overhead. The number of flights in and out of Heathrow had fallen off noticeably. They hurriedly loaded the car and started off, driving carefully along their street, past wheelie bins and spilled rubbish, out on to the main road into the eerie silence of a clear, bright autumn day.

Relieved to have escaped their local area, George turned to Sunny and said, "The APL have picked their moment well, capitalising on increasing political uncertainty. They pushed the button and melted away, presumably calculating that fear and mistrust would do the job of pulling society apart at the seams. But I can't help feeling they're waiting to apply some sort of killer blow."

They negotiated an army roadblock as they left the main road, driving on in pensive silence through country lanes. Derrick was reading the map and George drove slowly, leaning forward, alert for any signs of movement. The GPS and mobile phones had lost their signals, so they were technologically isolated. Rounding a corner, they came face-to-face with a magnificent stag, stood facing them in the middle of the single lane track. George stopped and turned to Sunny, "I wonder if the animals are aware of the turmoil going on in the world of humans?"

After a thirty-second staring match, the stag wandered off and they continued on their way, thankful for not meeting anyone or anything for the rest of their journey. The Willows Guesthouse came into view and they all cheered up, especially the gaming deprived boys, to take in the scene of a beautifully manicured lawn and weeping willows next to a babbling brook. "Isn't it quaint – the real England," drawled George as he pulled up in front of the two-storey, grey quarry-stoned building. "This'll be our sanctuary."

CHAPTER ELEVEN

GEORGE JUMPED OUT as a small man in an apron came bustling out to greet them, shaking hands and attempting an awkward man hug. "Hey! Baggy! Long time! It's great to see you again." The wee man blushed and stuttered, "G-George...great to see you too...and you've arrived safely. I'm so glad, and looking forward to hearing your take on the chaos and confusion. Come in and meet the wife."

They unloaded the luggage and made their way across the worn paving stone entrance into the oak-beamed reception area. "This is my wife, Molly, and our daughter, Desdemona." The attractive blond, teenage daughter was the tallest of the three, and the boys mumbled their names as they all shook hands. "Call me Dessie," she smiled warmly, fixing each of the visitors with a confident blue-eyed gaze.

They were shown to their rooms – the boys had to share a twin up in the attic, but didn't mind. George and Sunny had also agreed to share a room, and George smirked like the cat who'd got the cream as he bounced up and down on the massive king-sized four-poster bed. They had not slept together since the world went mad following the fateful terrorist party evening, and Sunny, closing the door, felt a need to make reparation, "George, about that night...I just want you to know that although I may have been attracted to Stevo's charm and, well, attractive build, I never thought for one minute that he would be a better partner than you. I just want you to know that you're the man I want to be with." George jumped off the bed and embraced the Indian beauty, kissing her hard on the lips, intoxicated by her sweet fragrance.

George and Arthur Bagshaw, a former Network Rail signal clerk known affectionately as 'Baggy', sat in the oak-panelled lounge with their coffees. Baggy was keen to hear George's story, and was suitably in awe at the tales of terrorists, pub bombings, the Thames Valley Defence Force versus the Anti-Poverty League, leading up to the terrible bombing of the Houses of Parliament, George's injury and the near-fatal injuries to Ken. George did so much talking, his coffee went cold. Molly appeared magically at his side and refreshed his mug.

While he was talking the other two families staying in the guesthouse came into the lounge to meet them. Brian and Jenny Oliver and their three young children were locals from the nearby village, and Tony and Violet Brown with two teenage children, Ben and Lucy, were from the town of Gloucester. Molly's mother, Pauline, also lived on the premises, and helped in the kitchen.

"Years of being attentive to guests has given her a sixth sense," Baggy said, leaning forward in his chair. "An incredible story, George, but now what happens? The country has descended into near anarchy with gangs of bandits roaming around and army roadblocks everywhere. Your email was one of the last we've received, and there's been no internet connection for a week. I've got you and two other families here, and we're running out of supplies. Also, we have random power cuts, so don't forget to get your candles and matches ready in your rooms where you can find them."

George sat back in the armchair and sipped his coffee. He didn't know what else to say. For the time being, he was just glad to be away from his housing estate. "I'll help you with a shopping run, but not for a day or two. I'm still recovering from my bomb blast injuries and, what with all the emotion and anxiety, and facing up to a street gang only this morning, I'm suddenly very tired." Baggy snapped back into host mode and stammered, "Y-y-yes of course, George, you must rest. This is the ideal place. You made the right decision coming here; the country air will do you and your family much good."

With that they shook hands and parted. George climbed the stairs to his room for an afternoon nap and Baggy shouted after him, "Don't forget – dinner is at seven!"

"THE TIME TO strike is now!" Peter Morris banged his fist on the table to emphasise the point and make sure he held the attention of the other six Anti-Poverty League executive committee members. "The partial success of our Westminster bombing has created an atmosphere of fear and uncertainty in the country, compounded by a constitutional crisis that has led to the farcical situation of the elderly and eccentric King Charles being dusted off to head-up a cabinet – or Privy Council as they like to call it – made up of the dubious land-owning elite. This has fallen right into our hands, as the public will see more clearly than ever the divisions in British society, with an effective return to an unelected royal ruler, whose instinct will be to protect the interests of the ruling class. The time is right to tip the population over the edge into outright revolution!"

The assembled group stood up and applauded.

Feisty Dervla could not contain herself, "Peter's right. Our job has only just begun. We must smash the power of the capitalist elite and forge a new society by whatever means possible!" More applause broke out. Peter looked over his faithful followers and knew he had their unswerving support. Putting his hands up for silence, he continued, "Okay, the next phase is to strike at the heart of the financial sector by disabling their computer systems. At the same time, we will also strike at the shaky interim government and disrupt as much of their means of operation as possible. To show us how this can be done, I'll hand over to Mr. Rob Wainright, our very own computer geek."

An unkempt, gangly, ginger-haired youth, with a wispy bumfluff beard, stood up and ambled over to a laptop and projector. "Errr...I've prepared a PowerPoint presentation to try and give you the overview of what I propose...without boring you with the technical detail." He jabbed at the keyboard and a stunning visual appeared on the screen, depicting a black city skyline melting beneath yellow rays of sunlight and the words 'Hello World' above in red dripping letters.

"Our cyber attack on the financial sector has been code-named, 'Hello World'." He saw he had their interest and moved to slide two - a complex diagram with text bubbles connected by arrows.

"Most large commercial and financial organisations have one major weakness – their over-reliance on computer systems linked to the World Wide Web. This is known as the 'Internet of Things' which is the interconnection of uniquely identifiable embedded computing devices within the existing Internet infrastructure." He looked out keenly over his audience, but saw from their blank expressions that he was way over their heads. "Errr...in simple layman's terms, this means that the world is run through computer programmes linked to the Internet, and that is their weakness. I've developed a computer virus that will be lodged into the web hub and radiate out through the Internet, targeting and disabling all computer systems that we have identified for our attack."

Jaws dropped as the enormity of his utterance hit home. After a few seconds Tommy spoke up, "Can I still use Facebook?" A ripple of laughter lightened the mood, and Rob continued, "For a while, yes, if you can get an internet connection of course, but in theory we could extend the reach of the virus to include social media, business websites and email providers. I've run tests and I believe there is a 90% chance it will work." He then spent ten minutes explaining a complex flow chart, but Dervla had already tuned out. Her mind was racing with the vision of a world thrown into chaos.

Peter took the floor again after Rob returned to his chair. "So there you have it," he said. "Rob has the computer equipment he needs to activate this bug right here, in our lead-lined computer room. The authorities would never be able to trace the signal back here, he tells me, so now all that remains is for us to pick the time for our next strike at the heart of our corrupt financial system and effectively take them back to a pre-Internet age. By the time we've finished with them they'll be calculating on the abacus! And now if you'll all leave us, I'd like some time with Dervla to discuss tactics. Thanks, and please respect our tight internal security, under Tommy's watchful eye. No one is to leave or attempt to contact the outside world. We remain in lockdown until we strike."

Peter and Dervla retired to his oak-paneled study. He approached his vintage jukebox and pressed some buttons. "Do you know why I called this estate 'Devil Gate Drive'?"

"No idea," Dervla said as she flopped into an armchair. "It combines two of my favourite interests," he continued, "70s rock music and the occult. This is one of my favourite tracks – *Devil Gate Drive* by Suzi Quattro. Do you believe in the Devil?" The rhythmic bass guitar and retro-drum beat sound filled the room, as Peter swayed awkwardly to the music whilst pouring a couple of brandies. "Oh yes," she replied with a mischievous grin, "I'm told I'm named after the Devil's daughter."

They clinked glasses in a toast to their devilish scheme. After a while Peter spoke, "Dervla, this Hello World computer attack is only one of the things I've got in mind. My sources tell me that King Charles has gone to Scotland to meet with his Privy Council and thrash out a manifesto for running the country. They'll be meeting at Balmoral tomorrow. I want you and Tommy to lead a snatch squad of no more than half a dozen hand-picked men to go up there and capture our illustrious king and bring him here. That should further destabilise things and have the security forces running around chasing their tails."

Dervla sat forward, "Peter! That's a marvellous idea! You do have a devious mind. Of course I'll do it. It'll be so much fun! Can we kill anyone?"

"Now, Dervla, the objective will be to snatch the King, not cause mayhem, although you may need to use necessary force when engaging with armed security officers. Use your judgement, but don't get tied down in a western-style shoot-out. First prize is a swift and low-key extraction with them not knowing he's gone. I've sketched out a draft plan, let's go over it..."

At dawn half a dozen four-by-fours drove out of Devil Gate Drive, each heading in different directions on tracks through dense woodland, with the intention of distracting the watching police so that Tommy and Dervla's team could slip away unnoticed. The Anti-Poverty League's field operatives, those that evaded police capture, had their instructions to cause mayhem and panic following the scheduled financial sector computer crash.

Primary targets for ground strikes to make the television news and terrify the country were the London Stock Exchange, Canary Wharf Tower, the NatWest Tower and the Bank of England – all symbols of the capitalist forces that had brought so much inequality to Western society and misery to most of the population. A statement had been prepared to send to all news organisations at the appropriate time.

Peter watched them go from the large bay window of his study, and checked his watch. It was seven o'clock and time for breakfast, then a final briefing with the computer team. Today was going to be a good day, the culmination of several months' work. It would be a day of reckoning for the capitalist West and the start of a new world order. He had named his computer virus 'Hello World' to indicate a new beginning. A new dawn for a post-capitalist age based on a fair and equitable society. The fact that this must be achieved through destruction and violence was a sad inevitability.

DEX SAT SULLENLY as he was lectured by one of his uncle's CIA operatives. "The Director is grateful for the feedback from you and your girlfriend and it does advance our understanding of the Anti-Poverty League, but as it stands it is still one big iceberg, with most of it unknown beneath the surface." Jim Garfield was the perfect spy - totally nondescript - Mister Average in every sense. After meeting him for a short while, you would have no recollection of what he looked like. Maybe this had kept him from being detected and had extended his shelf life as a field operative. Dex was bored by the lengthy briefing but kept tuned in to what was being said, waiting for the bit about what was expected of him. He gazed around the London office of his father's shadowy company, the walnut panels and gilt-framed portraits, out through the old sash windows to the grey building opposite.

"Here's the thing, Dex," Garfield continued. "We've had some information that this group is planning something big. The Limeys don't know what, or even where they're based, apart from staking out some English country mansion in the middle of nowhere. We've got one of our men up there, in Hertfordshire, and he thinks there is some kind of build-up of human and material resources going on. It's called Devil Gate Drive, and I want you to go up there to see if there's anything you can do to assist our man in the field. Your driver, Max, can assist with surveillance, and he's a useful guy to have around should any force be necessary. And take that cute girlfriend of yours along, but don't tell her anything. She could come in handy as she's a local."

CHAPTER TWELVE

DERVLA AND TOMMY hid in the bushes on the edge of a perfectly mown lawn, taking turns to look through a pair of binoculars at the elegant picture-perfect royal castle. Balmoral Estate is open to the public, with a steady pulse of visitors on the main approach, but they had carefully chosen an entry and exit point through a wooded area, with their vehicle parked thirty meters from their position, ready for a quick escape. Between them and the ivy-clad granite-walled building was fifty meters of lawn, and the occasional armed police officer, patrolling the outside of the building. They noticed movement in a downstairs window.

"It isn't so difficult after all..." King Charles drawled in his trademark laconic manner. He was seated at the head of an old oak dining table, covered with a white tablecloth, beneath the high beams of the Main Hall, surrounded by coats of arms and portraits. The expectant faces of his Privy Council stared at him, waiting for his presentation.

"You see, it really is quite simple. The British people want to feel valued again, and we know how to deliver a better, eco-friendly quality of life."

The country was still getting used to the recently declared interim Government of National Unity, headed by King Charles III. The maverick royal, now in his seventies, had ignored discredited politicians and unpopular business leaders in pulling together a cabinet of odd-ball intellectuals and do-gooders to lead the country to their idealised vision of the future. Charles had recruited mainly from his own charity, The Prince's Trust, and from other interest groups, including architects, who would help articulate a clear path to realising his progressive ideas for low-cost, eco-friendly transport systems and housing, in addition to renewable energy and recycled materials for industry and agriculture.

Charles had sat on the sidelines for most of his life, waiting for a ceremonial role as a powerless constitutional monarch. He had been mocked for his views and outlandish ideas of an alternative future for his subjects, and had dared to dream of a day when he would have a mandate to paint his stunning vision on such a broad canvas. That day had now arrived.

"The future's so bright, I've got to wear sunglasses," he drawled, eliciting polite laughter from the eager faces around the table. He pulled at his shirt cuffs and toyed with a bejewelled cufflink.

"The people have simply had enough of a small minority of greedy capitalists driving down their earnings and reducing their quality of life. We have been handed this opportunity, rather unexpectedly, to redress the balance and give our people a leg up, as it were. The time has come for a readjustment of values in our hard-pressed country – a new equitable and clean air society! The Lord Chief Justice will be joining us tomorrow to advise on the legality of us being able to enact new laws, and to discuss the bills that were before the last parliament, including the proposed privatisation of the police force and the armed forces. We can debate those in the morning and decide if we want to go ahead and pass them into law. As her father and I are old school friends, I doubt there will be any problems. Quentin, can you go through the three-point plan?" Charles sat to a ripple of applause, a self-satisfied smirk on his face.

A short balding man in a tweed jacket pushed his chair back and shuffled over to a flip chart, to deliver a very low-tech, some might say traditional, presentation.

He half-turned and bowed slightly before clearing his throat.

"Erm...Your Majesty... fellow council members. As you can see from this chart, we intend to propose a three-point plan for the country as follows:

Firstly, we need to return to self-sufficiency by producing our own food and the manufactured goods most in demand by consumers and industry. By doing this we should also achieve full employment, even to the extent of reintroducing a form of National Service for early school-leavers and the unemployed, who will be incentivised to work for their money.

Glances were exchanged, and Charles nodded his assent. Quentin paused and eyed the group, looking for a reaction. Bright eyes and earnest smiles let him know he was on safe ground.

"Secondly, we plan a radical overhaul of the property market. The private rental market will be abolished and the compulsory purchase of investment properties will be introduced. A Property Board will be set up to administer the acquisition and building of properties and the rental of accommodation at fixed and affordable rates. Those currently making a living as private landlords will be compensated and encouraged to find alternative livelihoods. The sector has simply gotten out of hand and must be restored to affordable rents of modernised properties. Paying less for rents will free up more disposable income, and will improve the standard of living of the tenants.

Existing housing stock will be modernised, and a programme of building modern, environmentally friendly, energy efficient housing, designed by the king and his royal architects, will be announced. We plan, over time, to shift the balance in the property market away from private ownership to high-quality, low-cost rentals."

Applause broke out around the table, and some members of the Privy Council shifted excitedly in their seats. Quentin flipped over the chart and continued.

"Thirdly, opinion polls conducted earlier in the year, suggest there is much support in the country to renationalise all energy and utility companies, bringing them once again under state control, with proper investment and lower costs to the public and industry. We will not nationalise industry, but we will regulate it and support it more effectively, with proper school-to-work apprentice and training schemes."

"Once these policies are in place, we will turn our attention to the future and a new constitution. We have already set up a constitutional review committee and tasked them with drawing up a draft constitution for the United Kingdom, based on it becoming a federal republic with a president, supported by an executive committee, overseeing three regional parliaments for England, Scotland and Wales. King Charles agrees that the monarch should no longer be the head of state, and the Royal Family will be privatised as a public listed company in which members of the public will be invited to buy shares. The Royal Family Plc, as it were."

Sporadic, uncertain applause rang out from half of those around the table, and one hand went up.

"Yes, Jeremy," Quentin said.

"Erm, you said there would be three regional parliaments for England, Wales and Scotland, but no mention of Northern Ireland. What of them?"

Quentin paused and turned to the ageing monarch, who pushed his bony knuckles hard on the arms of his chair and stood up. He moved carefully to the front of the table and laid his hands on the white tablecloth.

"Thank you, Quentin, for an excellent and concise presentation of our main policies. Please flip to the next page of the presentation." A map of the British Isles appeared with the main island shown in the colours of the Union Flag and the whole of Ireland in green, with some arrows and bubbles containing graphic representations of family groups dotted around.

Charles glanced at it and carried on, "On the question of Northern Ireland, I can tell you all, in confidence, that my call to the Irish Premier, Mister Murphy, has yielded a favourable response. He is willing to enter into secret negotiations concerning the transfer of sovereignty of the troublesome province of Northern Ireland to the Republic of Ireland. I have come up with a solution to resistance from Ulster Protestants, the majority of whom have Scottish heritage, namely the construction of a purpose-built modern town in Scotland so they can return, en masse, to their roots. We will call this 'Operation Truman Show'."

He beamed at his acolytes who responded with warm applause. There would be no opposition from this carefully-selected group of sycophants, basking in the warm glow of their self-righteous mission to save the floundering country and move it towards a secular, modern society, defined by science, technology and their code of human decency. The proposal to ditch Northern Ireland didn't trouble anyone or raise any eyebrows. They could get used to making sweeping decisions without consulting those who would be affected. It was, after all, a state of national emergency.

JUST THEN THERE was an explosion from the corridor outside and the sound of raised voices and running feet. The door burst open and a security guard was thrown into the room, landing on his backside on the plush royal carpet. Four gunmen stepped into the room, wearing combat fatigues and black balaclavas, black eyes gleaming with menace. One of them addressed himself directly to King Charles, speaking in a broad West Yorkshire accent: "I am Abu Akbar from the British Islamic Brotherhood. I've come for you, Charles Windsor. We've heard about your plans to remove Muslims from this country, and we are starting the fight back. Right here. Right now!"

"Errr...now look here, my man..." Charles stammered, as he rose from his chair. The gunman pushed him down and stood over him. "Don't you 'my man' me! I'm a British citizen wiv as much rights as all youse around dis table. Don't try and patronise me or deny your evil scheme. I can see it all there on the chart! Mo, shut the door!"

He pointed to the flip chart with the heading 'Operation Truman Show', with a map of the British Isles showing an arrow indicating the movement of people from Northern Ireland to Scotland, clearly choosing to only see the arrow and graphic of a group of people, and not the geography. His colleague kicked the feet of the groaning security man away from the door, closed and locked it, standing with his back to it and slowly swinging the barrel of his automatic weapon over the terrified privy counsellors.

"You can't push King Charles like that! Clearly you didn't pay much attention in geography class or you would see that..." were the last words uttered by Quentin, who had plucked up the courage from somewhere to front-up to the terrorist leader. The women screamed and the men groaned as a ripple of muted machine gun fire cut him down. Red plumes of blood stained his white shirt as he fell backwards on his chair, a shocked look on his face, framed in his moment of death, before rolling onto the carpet.

"We're not here to play games! Let that be a warning to you! You will do exactly what I say, or meet the same fate.

Now, on your feet!" The horrified group stood up and were corralled into the corner of the room, along with the security man. Abu Akbar moved to the big sash windows and opened up one of them.

From the woods, Dervla and Tommy viewed the sudden movement in the room and what looked like flashes of gunfire with heightened interest.

"Looks like someone's beaten us to it," Tommy said, as he handed the binoculars to Dervla.

"Damn!" she said. "They've just opened a window and I can see one of them wearing a balaclava." They continued to study the side of the building, and noticed an armed security guard sauntering along, heading for the open window, unaware of what was happening.

"Quick! I want you all out of this window, now!" A commotion had started in the corridor outside, and there were shouts and hammering on the door. One of the gunmen took a few steps away from the door, turned, and sprayed a volley of bullets into it, splintering the wood and causing momentary silence on the other side. A startled guard outside the open window was silenced with a single pistol shot through the forehead from the calm and determined Abu Akbar. Charles and his counsellors made a hasty and undignified exit through the window, helped by a few pushes and prods from gun barrels.

Outside, a large removals van had been backed up on the lawn, and the tailgate was down. On either side stood two similarly armed gunmen, who indicated that the group should get in. A fascinating scene was unfolding before Dervla and Tommy. They saw two armed police officers run onto the lawn, fatally hesitating to fire their weapons as the King and his counsellors hurried across the grass. A hail of machine gun fire cut them down. The element of surprise was still with the terrorists, but not for long. They closed up the back of the truck; two dived in the back with the hostages and three leapt into the driver's cabin. They drove off towards the rear of the Balmoral Estate, bouncing along a gravel single track road. The lawn was soon alive with shouting and gesticulating police officers, running security guards and barking dogs.

Dervla and Tommy had seen enough. To add to the confusion, they had noticed another group observing events from the woods near them, also watching through binoculars.

"Bloody Scottish nationalists," Tommy said, "we better get moving in case they're also thinking what we're thinking. We need to head them off before they leave the estate and take the hostages!" Dervla's eyes danced with excitement. She put her hand on his arm, "No, wait!"

"What is it?" Tommy replied.

"Let's follow the Scottish nationalists and see if they confront the Islamists. Maybe we could take advantage of a shoot-out to grab King Charles." Tommy grinned, and they made their way back to their Range Rover and two armed colleagues. They drove carefully through the forest until they spotted the vehicle they took to belong to their rivals, and followed them as they headed on a course to intercept the removals van before it left the royal estate. It took barely five minutes before they reached the main track, and they hung back in the tree line as their rivals took up their ambush position behind a small hill before the exit gate.

They deployed themselves, Tommy and his backup armed and ready behind trees, and Dervla behind the wheel of the vehicle, as they heard the furniture van approach, heading for a road block ambush just over a rise in the road. Sure enough, the startled driver instinctively applied his foot to the brake, and the van skidded from side to side before stopping in a cloud of dust. The Scottish nationalists marched towards the van, and sprayed the driver's cab with bullets. The rear gate was dropped and the other two kidnappers emerged to return fire. Tommy burst from cover and, taking advantage of the lingering dust cloud, was able to reach the back of the van unseen. The two jihadis had taken cover and were busy shooting at the Scots, as Tommy entered the back of the van where the cowering captives looked up in a mixture of fear and expectation at what looked like a British soldier in khaki fatigues.

"King Charles, come with me," he commanded, and the elderly man obeyed without hesitation. He signalled to Dervla who drove up in seconds, and they all jumped in and sped away, with Tommy throwing smoke bombs to cover their escape, laughing at the surprised and forlorn looks of the abandoned hostages and the gazumped terrorists. Dervla drove madly towards a forest track as Tommy put new coordinates into the GPS.

"I'll guide you through country roads until we RV with the chopper," he said.

BIRDS ROWING OUTSIDE his window was the first sound George heard as he woke up and lay on his back, on a ridiculously soft king-sized mattress, staring at the Tudor ceiling and a Homebase imitation chandelier hanging from it. He was in the Willows Guesthouse in a rural part of the Cotswolds, somewhere in Gloucestershire and far enough away from his council estate. He turned to look at the sleeping beauty next to him. He had made the right decision bringing them here.

George wandered over to the window and surveyed the scene of tranquil beauty lying below a thin veil of early morning mist. The green mown lawn led to a row of willow trees, weeping branches bowing down to a babbling brook. A squirrel ran from tree to tree and a hedgehog slowly snuffled near the rose bushes. He set up his new tripod and digital camera, snapping pictures of animals and birds. He turned to see Sunny was now awake, stretching and rubbing her eyes as a shaft of sunlight played across the bed. "They have hedgehogs here!" he said enthusiastically, "I haven't seen one for ages!"

Sunny yawned and sat up, taking in the room in natural light.

George continued, "Yes, my dear, believe it. We are in the heart of merry England, away from the concrete jungle and roaming gangs of the Runnymede Estate. At least here we can rest and re-appraise our situation, as the country crumbles around us."

He lay back on the bed and invited her to shower first. His thoughts turned to the missing member of his family, his daughter Essie. She was still staying at the Ritz with Dexter. He hoped they were safe in central London. There was no mobile signal and the internet was down, well, at least those sites used by the public. Messaging was a problem. He would ask Baggy over breakfast about means of communication and if the telephone lines were still open. He shouted through to the bathroom, "I hope the king can calm the rioters and steady the ship!"

"Ehh?" Sunny replied, looking round the corner at him, her mouth full of toothpaste.

"I'm saying I hope the king can restore order, because it looks like the terrorists have achieved their first objective of destabilising the country and forcing people to stay indoors out of fear. It's amazing how quickly things can descend into lawlessness and anarchy."

"What will be their second objective?" Sunny asked.

"Well, their second objective will be to take power. A full-scale revolution, like Castro in Cuba."

"Surely that can't happen here; besides the army and police are too strong," she replied.

George paused before adding, "We've seen how determined, ruthless and organised the Anti-Poverty League is. They could join with other groups to bring this country to its knees, and then seize power by means of a *coup d'etat*. We're teetering on the edge, and now have our own King Lear – the eccentric King Charles – to rely on for salvation. God help us."

ESSIE TURNED TO Dex as they sat reading newspapers over breakfast.

"What do your security guys have to say about the declaration of a state of emergency in the UK and an interim government led by the king?"

He put down the *New York Times* and said, "It's made the front page news in the States. Here, have a look." He showed her the front page: 'Britain Restores Monarchy'.

"I guess they think it's quaint," she said, buttering a fresh bagel.

"Well, with the bandwagon rolling for a second term for Donald Trump, there could be a couple of very eccentric leaders of our two countries. Boy, what an interesting meeting that would be!"

"I thought you were all for Trump? Now you're calling him eccentric," Essie said absentmindedly.

"Yeah, well, we're seeing the UK fall apart all around us over unpopular policies that favour the rich and screw everyone else. Trump is re-running on the same ticket. With the EU in perpetual crisis, the whole of the western world could collapse. Hell, we could all be speaking Chinese soon."

"As long as they still make bagels," she said, popping a bit with jam into her mouth.

"I doubt it. It'll be boiled rice in the morning and fried rice for dinner," he grinned. "Changing the subject to more immediate matters, my dad's advisors have asked me to go up to Hertfordshire to check out someone they're interested in. It could be fun, and a change of scenery. We've been cooped up in this hotel for two days. Would you like to come along?"

"Is it dangerous?" she asked pensively. "I don't think you should get sucked into any covert investigation stuff, Dex. Look what happened to my dad. Leave it to the professionals."

"It's not like that. We'll be with a guy who does all the snooping around. We'll just book into a nice quaint English B&B and see if we can help in a very low-key way. Go for walks in the countryside. Come on, it'll be a hoot."

She agreed and casually requested another shopping trip to Selfridges for appropriate outdoor clothes. She had finished her first year exams and had free time, although in a state of emergency with armed police and soldiers everywhere, she didn't feel very free.

CHAPTER THIRTEEN

IN THE TINY Cotswolds village of Stow-on-the-Wold, George and Baggy sat behind the wheel of an old Land Rover Defender, surveying the quiet street outside the local supermarket. No one was about, and they could see a long way in both directions along the old Roman road – once called the Fosse Way, but now the A429. Derrick and Ravi had come along to help with the trolley dash.

Baggy nervously opened his door, "Come on, let's do it. Remember the plan – George, you stand by the door with my shotgun, and I'll supervise the lads collecting what they can find. The store manager is a friend, and will accept a cash payment. Let's go!" They approached the supermarket and saw that the door was locked and barricaded. Baggy tapped on the window and a man's face appeared. He eyed the group and opened the door.

"Hi Baggy, good to see you're safe and well. Please come in. Cash sale only, mind."

"No problem, I've got plenty of cash. My friend George will stand outside and keep watch...I'll go round with the two lads. Any trouble?"

"Oh yes...there's two gangs who've been fighting for control of the village. The Romans control the area to the east of the road, and the Drones control the west. They play a game of hide and seek with our small police force, now down to just three. They've stopped responding to call outs. I've managed to stop the gangs from looting by paying protection money and supplies to each, and they've agreed to come on alternate days! Sorry, the prices have all gone up as a result. It's a nightmare. Some of my regulars have been mugged and had their shopping stolen. It's a good thing you brought some support and have parked right outside. I'll see you to your vehicle in case either of the gangs shows up. Times are bad, and I don't know when I'll be re-supplied, some things have already run out..."

Baggy, alarmed by his account, cut him short and pushed past, keen to get started. "We'll be as quick as we can," he said, as he ushered the boys in with a trolley each. "Stick to what's on your lists boys, let's go!" It was as much fun as the teenagers had had in days. They had to resort to reading and walks in the countryside since they were rationed to an hour a day on their tablets. No internet updates, though, only what was saved on their devices. They were re-playing the same games. Times were indeed hard. Baggy negotiated a price for paraffin heaters with lights, and made sure to buy several packets of candles. Power cuts had become regular and for longer periods of time.

They paid up and wished the store manager good luck, loaded the supplies into the vehicle, aware that they were being watched. "I don't like this," moaned Baggy, as he fired up the ignition. "Now we have to run the gauntlet of a trip to the petrol station for diesel and paraffin. Stay alert." They drove slowly along the road and approached the only filling station. Baggy stopped abruptly fifty yards short, as two hooded men with scarves over their mouths stepped into the road. One held a shotgun and the other a baseball bat. George spoke first, "Well, we can either approach them and negotiate for fuel, or turn around and head home. They'll have seen us coming out of the supermarket and know we're loaded with supplies. What do you want to do?"

Baggy sat tense and motionless, his knuckles were white as he gripped the steering wheel. "Maybe we should withdraw and make a separate visit for fuel another day...we can't risk the safety of the boys and the supplies."

With that, he put the car into reverse and they moved away from the two men, who suddenly were joined by two more. After a fairly laborious three-point turn and they were off, driving out of the village and along country lanes, hopefully a safe five miles' distance to the security of the guesthouse.

"We'll need to review our defences when we get back," George intoned in a low serious voice. They lapsed into a pensive silence as they bounced along country lanes, passing no living soul on the drive to the Willows Guesthouse.

"THANKS GEORGE," MUMBLED a sweating Baggy, "I'm not cut out for leadership and moved here for a peaceful life. It's a godsend you being here to organise us, particularly with your experience of dealing with terrorists...the Browns and the Olivers have both told me the same. We're all worried about these gangs roaming the area and up to no good."

George was a reluctant leader. A shy youth, he had joined Railtrack straight from school on an apprenticeship scheme. He had worked his way up from signalman to operations manager over a thirty-year career. A key moment had been when he was offered promotion to the ranks of middle management, an offer he thought long and hard about before accepting. This required taking an internal management training course, and he had to endure the jibes of his workmates as he left them behind, effectively crossing an invisible line on the floor to join the much-mocked bosses.

One of the biggest personal challenges he faced was to overcome his crushing shyness and reluctance to address a group of more than two people. The management trainer identified this as a barrier to his otherwise smooth transition, and worked with him on techniques to improve his self-confidence. He had been an awkward public speaker, but was determined to conquer his fears, and in time he was able to address a room full of workers on topics ranging from health and safety to signals procedures. His secondment to Zambia Railways had also helped build up his self-esteem. They treated him as an expert in all things railway, and he became that person, returning to the UK with a self-confidence that surprised some.

Now, sitting in the lounge of the Willows Guesthouse, he looked up from his reflections at the expectant faces of eight adults and their children. They were waiting for someone to organise them - to tell what they must do. The reporting of the trip to the village for supplies and the failure to buy fuel had unsettled everyone. A siege mentality took hold.

"How do you know they won't come here? They must have recognised Baggy and the Land Rover...what are we going to do if an armed gang turn up?" Mister Oliver spoke for the frightened group.

The look of helplessness in Baggy's eyes told George that he must take charge. A reluctant leader, but a leader nonetheless. "OK...whilst we still have mains electricity we can continue as normal, cooking in the kitchen and eating fresh food from the fridge. We should stock up the freezer as much as possible. We'll all eat together and eat the same meal. Molly can prepare a meal plan. When the power goes we can defrost what's in the freezer and cook outside on the barbeque. The ladies can help Molly and Pauline with food preparation, the vegetable plot, storage and foraging in the woods. In the future we may need to consider hunting for meat. I know this is gender stereotyping, so please speak up if you have other skills or want to do something else.

The old lady spoke up, "I know how to make charcoal from wood, if one of the boys helps me. We will need it for cooking and heating the house."

"That's great, Pauline," George said. "Let's start by collecting firewood and prepare the oil lamps. Baggy, you should make sure your generator is in working order. On defence, I think we need to look to strengthening the perimeter fence, dig a ditch and set up a guard hut by the lane. We only have one shotgun and one pistol, so we should think about other weapons."

"I have a bow and arrow!" Dessie squealed.

"Okay, that may come in handy for hunting. Let's get started. All the men come with me on a tour of the perimeter." They brightened up with something to do and someone to lead them. Sunny was not interested in the company of the other women, and along with the three teenage boys, volunteered to be in the guarding group with the men, giving a respectable team of eight.

George organised them into two groups: one for digging ditches and making an earth rampart and the other for building a guard hut. He returned to the house and decided to make a phone call whilst there was still a line. His attempts to call Essie proved fruitless, and so he tried calling Inspector Wilson, finally getting through after several attempts.

"Hello George," he droned in a tired monotone, "glad to hear you're safe and out in the countryside. Things are bad here in London and in most of the towns and cities around the country. We are struggling to contain the rising violence and crime. Supplies to supermarkets have become erratic, as have electronic payments due to weak internet connection, and the sudden shift to cash sales has emptied cash point machines which are not being replenished. It's a mess. The army have taken over telephone and mobile communications and monitor all media output. As the Americans would say, it's a clusterfuck."

"Is there any news of Ken and the Anti-Poverty League?" George asked.

"Yeah, we have an insider who has told us that they are preparing for a major operation, but we don't know what. We have Peter Morris's country house staked out. They all appear to be in there. We're waiting for armed support before swooping on them. Oh, and Ken is on the mend and should soon be out of intensive care."

After a moment's pause, Wilson continued, "George, if for any reason the APL manage to escape us, or we have them cornered, can I send a car for you? I might need your help again to identify them, and your ideas might come in handy as you know as much about them as any of us."

George took a few seconds before replying, "I'm not sure I'd want to get involved again, I'm still carrying wounds to my left side, and I feel as stiff as the proverbial board. This lot here have elected me leader for organising the defence of the guesthouse, would you believe. Although this country retreat is pleasant for me and my family, it's far from secure."

Wilson laughed. "I guess you're now qualified as an anti-terror consultant. There's no security anywhere, George, you might be better off with us...think about it, I'll be in touch. Make a note of my short wave radio frequency and call sign, just in case the phones go down."

Details were recorded, and George came off the phone feeling anxious again. Maybe there was no getting away from what they had started as the Thames Valley Defence Force. Perhaps the destinies of himself and Sunny were irrevocably tied up with the fortunes of the terror group, bound together in a macabre dance of death. He would discuss the conversation later with Sunny; but for now, there was work to be done.

BRITAIN HAD ALREADY descended into an economic and social crisis following the attack on the Houses of Parliament and the flight of many companies in the financial, IT and other sectors to other countries. The stock market had plummeted and as austerity demonstrations descended into rioting and looting, the numbers of people going to work in towns and cities had dropped alarmingly. The internet, mobile and landline connections and electricity supply had become erratic, and for those working from home things were far from easy.

In the computer room in Devil Gate Drive, Peter checked his watch as he stood behind computer geek Rob, waiting for news from Dervla and also of the Canary Wharf bomb planted by his second team in London Docklands. This would be the catalyst for starting the Hello World internet virus. He had mused for days on the possible consequences of computer systems linked to the internet – the Internet of Things – crashing all at once. Corporations would grind to a standstill, production would halt, transport systems grounded, governments made defenceless and at risk of attack by their enemies. He would effectively be pressing the reboot button on the entire world – maybe low-tech societies would thrive? Corporate USA would be brought down, making them more insular and paranoid than usual, forcing a rethink in foreign policy and rebalancing power bases and relations. His reverie was broken by the sound of an approaching helicopter.

Tommy and Dervla arrived triumphantly in Peter's personal helicopter with the captured King Charles. Peter beamed at the sight of the bowed and frightened king, looking dejected and forlorn in a mud-stained blue Armani suit.

"Welcome to my home, Your Majesty!" he said, making a mock bow to the king. "Please come into my study for some refreshments."

"Look here! I don't know who you are, but you must release me at once! The country will be in uproar. They have suffered enough disturbances already. This is simply monstrous!"

Peter couldn't hide his glee, and cackled like a Bond villain, "My dear King Charles, I doubt very much that the army and security forces will make public your disappearance. I'm sure your son, General Harry Wales, is frantically searching for you as we speak. As you say, the country is already teetering on the brink of complete collapse of civil order. In fact, it's my self-appointed mission to push it over the edge! Ha ha!"

He guided Charles, Dervla and Tommy into his study and closed the door. "Tommy, can you please attend to the king? Take him to the bedroom we've prepared and order him some tea and snacks from the kitchen. I need to talk to Dervla in private." With that he bowed to the unhappy old man and closed the door of his study to be alone with his partner in anarchy.

"My dear, let me congratulate you!" He hugged her warmly. "Tell me all." Dervla recounted the snatch of King Charles and his privy counsellors by a group of Muslim jihadis, and the successful interception of their getaway van. There followed a brief shoot-out, during which one of their group – Michael O'Brien, a friend of hers – had been killed, along with all six of the Muslim snatch squad. She did not know who they were or where they came from. They released the surviving privy counsellors and took Charles to the waiting helicopter.

"An incredible story!" Peter said. "There has been no news of the kidnapping of the king, nor mention of any Muslim jihadi group. The army and security services must be controlling all information and are keeping potentially destabilising events away from the public. We are unable to hack into their messaging communications. All I know is they have us surrounded and are probably planning to come in when they are reinforced. We must look to our defences."

"Where are we with Hello World?" Dervla asked.

"I'm waiting to hear from Gerry and Team Two at Canary Wharf. Any time now, he should set off a bomb in the underground car park, a big enough explosion to rock the building and cause a panicked evacuation." He smiled at her, and they enjoyed a moment of reflective conceit.

Police surveillance teams outside had certainly noticed the arrival of a helicopter, but it was not as yet connected with the kidnap of King Charles. There were slightly confusing reports of Muslim terrorists and a second group who killed the first in a shoot-out. They had been left with a puzzle to solve – who had spirited the elderly king away from the shoot-out between the Muslim jihadis and Scottish Nationalists? Inspector Wilson had his own ideas, and was still waiting for army support before entering the country house grounds. He knew there was a vacuum in British politics that had caused a paralysis in the chain of command, thus slowing the response time of the combined defence and security forces. For the time being, at least, the police were still responsible for basic law and order, although cutbacks over the past thirty-odd years had severely reduced their numbers and resources.

"We are reaping what we have sown," he mumbled to no one in particular, as he inspected the tyre tracks through the woods behind the grounds of the country house, and knew that some of the terrorists had given them the slip. He knew they were planning something big, but his inside informant, a lowly cleaner, had not provided any details. He needed fresh thinking on the matter and resolved to call George to join him in a team to combat the terrorists – a wistful smile crossed his thin lips, and he said out loud, to a puzzled police officer, "An anti-Anti-Poverty League Team, that's what we need, Jones."

The young police woman responded, "But Sir, the two 'antis' cancel each other out, so you're left with a Poverty League Team. Does that mean we're batting for the Capitalists?"

Wilson was irked by her witty remark, "Alright Jones, I'll do the jokes if you don't mind. Now tell me what type of vehicle made those tracks." He wondered if sympathy for the aims of the APL was undermining the commitment of some of his people. Are they motivated to try and catch these villains when so many of their family and friends are suffering from increasing poverty? No more of this. "Remember who pays your wages, Jones, now get on with it."

THE WILLOWS GUESTHOUSE had been without electricity for two nights when they came. The three boys – Derrick, Ravi and Ben – ran along the moonlit corridor, knocking on doors to awaken the startled residents. George and Sunny quickly pulled on their clothes, lit their oil lamps, and hurried downstairs to the lounge where the others were collecting.

"What's going on?" George asked, as he entered the room.

Derrick answered first, "There's a gang outside, Dad, walking down the lane. I was on guard duty with Mister Oliver. He's still out there, keeping an eye on them, whilst I came in to raise the alarm." George noticed that Derrick was wearing Sunny's Woolf Head Security shirt and cap.

"Good boy," George said, "and that uniform suits you. You look like a proper guard." Derrick beamed shyly, clearly pleased at his dad's approval. George spoke to the group: "Let's divide ourselves into the two groups we had before. The outside defence group, come with me. The inside group should remain here with Baggy and look to fortify the house as best as possible."

They divided into two, after some hugging and kissing, and the male group with Sunny made ready to leave. Dessie wanted to join them, holding her bow and arrow, as she had become close to Derrick, but her mother pulled her back, "You stay here with me, my love. I need your good eyes and knowledge of the house."

George clutched Baggy's old army service revolver and led his group of seven outside. The full moon lit their way across the lawn to the makeshift guard hut. A tense and visibly relieved Brian Oliver, clutching the barrel of the shotgun tightly, made his whispered report.

"There are about a dozen of them, down the lane. They've stopped in the lay-by up there and sent scouts out into the woods behind the guesthouse. They're definitely checking us out."

George thought for a moment. "Right, we can assume that they know about us and they've come to plunder us. We can either wait for them to move first, or we can hit them with a surprise attack. It seems to me that there's no way of avoiding conflict, so my preferred line of action is to give ourselves an advantage by attacking first. What do you all think?"

There was a brief murmured discussion, reaching a broad consent for an attack.

"We don't know how well armed they are, or how good at fighting... we will be putting ourselves at risk of getting injured or worse..." George held up his hand and put a stop to Brian's worrying. "Yes, there are risks, and we need to be clear about the repercussions of using force. People will get hurt. But this is one of those rare occasions when we must act decisively in our defence, or our families will be in danger. I say we attack with clubs and staffs aimed at their bodies and knees; get them down, overpower them and tie them up. Brian, are you up to firing that shotgun if needs be?"

"No... not really... I've never fired one and I don't think I could shoot anyone."

Tony Brown steeped forward and took the shotgun from him, saying, "I'll take that, I've shot rabbits and the like, but never at a person."

"Alright," George said, "we'll try not to kill anyone, but if they fight back we may have to wound them, especially anyone who is armed, so be ready. We'll walk up the edge of the lane in single file and then rush them, each take a different target and focus on knocking them to the ground, and then Sunny and the boys will follow up with the strips of rope and duct tape and bind up their hands, OK?"

"Then what will do with them?" Brian whispered.

George paused for a second. "We can put all captured prisoners in the tool shed. Come on, let's go."

They approached cautiously and crouched ten yards away from their targets, just out of the glow of their makeshift camp fire. They were chatting away, and George counted seven. On his signal they rushed in, yelling to cause panic and confusion. George felt obliged to lead by example and bashed the nearest man on the head with the butt of his pistol and he fell to the ground. The others took encouragement and each selected a target to attack. George moved onto a startled-looking young man, about the same age as Derrick. After a moment's hesitation, he opted to bear-hug the youth and wrestle him to the ground. Ravi quickly appeared to bind his hands. In less than a minute it was over. Five bound men on the ground, with two having fled into the woods. George crouched menacingly over the frightened youth, shaking him by his arms, and demanded, "How many of you are there?"

"Aaargh!" He cried, more in fear than in pain, "Don't hurt us, mister! There are only twelve of us; we're just looking around the woods, that's all!"

George replied, "Yeah, well, you've come too close to our guesthouse. I don't think it's a coincidence you've come here is it? What were you planning on doing with us?"

The man replied, "Nothing! Honest! We were just looking for food, that's all!"

"I'm not having that," George growled. "You've plenty of food up at the supermarket in town."

"No Sir! The other gang, the Romans, have taken it over and driven us out of town. We're the Drones...now living in the woods. We weren't going to hurt you, honest!"

They were pulled to their feet and marched down the lane and back to the guesthouse. The tool shed was cleared out and they were put into there, and a padlock secured the door. George divided his group into two and they patrolled around the house, looking for the missing four or five gang members. The moonlight favoured them as they were now the hunters. Before long, and after a brief and noisy struggle, they had apprehended three others and put them into the prison shed. George set two to guard, with Derrick and Ravi enthusiastically volunteering. They lit a fire and patrolled around the edge of the garden, peering into the darkness and throwing stones. Computer games now forgotten; this was the most fun they had had for ages.

The triumphant heroes returned to the house, to be greeted by the happy group inside. There had been an attempted break-in at the kitchen door, but they had not succeeded, and soon melted away into the night when the commotion started on the lane. For the moment they were safe, and George and Sunny sat in the comfy armchairs in the lounge and allowed themselves to be served with hot drinks and scones, satisfied with their victory in the Battle of the Willows Guesthouse.

"I'm guessing that the Drones are the weaker of the two gangs – let's hope we don't get a visit from the Romans!" George said, drawing a laugh from the assembled group and relieving some of the tension. Baggy produced a book on the Romans in Britain and showed the youngsters a coloured sketch of legionnaires marching along Watling Street.

"Now I know how the Britons felt when the Romans cleared off and left them defenceless in mid-fifth century," he quipped, as Molly and Dessie brought in another tray of hot chocolate.

"They had to learn to defend themselves," Brian said bluntly, "just like we're doing."

CHAPTER FOURTEEN

A CHAUFFEUR-DRIVEN Mercedes car edged its way through an army checkpoint. Dex grinned at the Territorial Army captain and described their business as 'visiting friends'. They were booked into The Fox and Hounds pub and guesthouse. Their driver followed the blue line on his GPS along the High Street in the picturesque Hertfordshire village of Much Hadham and arrived at the seventeenth century coaching inn. Essie noted the swinging sign; a picture of a fox being chased by a huntsman and a pack of hounds, and wondered if the terrorists were being as hotly pursued by the forces of law and order. She watched their moody and somewhat muscular driver, Max, carry their bags in one trip into reception. Do all Americans work out?

They checked into their rooms, the big men making the wooden floorboards creak noisily as their bulky frames and bowed heads squeezed up the narrow staircase and filled up the claustophobic upstairs passage.

"Gee, folks were small in olden times," Max said, as he continued past their room to a single room at the far end of the corridor. They were in a double suite overlooking the High Street. Dex was pleased, and did that thing that men do – threw himself on the double bed and bounced up and down.

"Do ya think this is the honeymoon suite?" he laughed, winking at her. Essie smiled and did that thing that women do and checked out the bathroom. Satisfied, she moved in with her toilet and make-up bags.

"You unpack honey, I just need a quick word with Max," he said and hurried out of the room.

MOLLY JUMPED AT the unexpected and almost forgotten sound of the phone ringing. She rushed to pick up the receiver.

"Hello?" she asked with trepidation.

"This is Inspector Wilson, may I please speak with George Osborne?" the deep monotone voice demanded. She carried the receiver outside to George, who was busy digging a trench along the outer edge of their once beautiful lawn.

"George! It's for you!" she trilled. Thinking it might be Essie, he wiped soil from his hands as he climbed out of the muddy hole. He was slightly disappointed to hear the dull voice of the Inspector.

"We're sending a car for you and your family, George. The APL has struck in Canary Wharf and at the same time financial sector computer systems have been severely disrupted by a virus. Our sources tell us that this is the work of the terror group, and to make matters worse, a prominent figure has been kidnapped, and we suspect their involvement. I can't say too much on the phone, but we think we have their leaders surrounded and I want you here to join my team of advisers."

George was suitably alarmed at the list of bad news. "But Inspector, we're under siege here from local gangs. Last night we literally did battle with one gang and managed to capture most of them and now have them locked up in an outhouse! I'm not sure I can leave these people to fend for themselves..."

Wilson felt obliged to offer a solution to get his man. "OK, George, I'll send a detachment of three armed men to cover for you in your absence, and we'll even take away your prisoners...how's that?"

"Well, I guess it could work. Can you also bring supplies of food, water, diesel, kerosene, a first aid kit and anything else you can think of?"

"Yes, George, be packed and ready to go this evening, we should be there in four to five hours."

The deal was done, and George gave the bad news of his imminent departure to a crestfallen Baggy, Molly, Brian and Tony. Derrick and Dessie exchanged miserable looks.

"But why do I have to go, Dad? Can't I stay here to help out?" he whined. Ravi also pleaded with his mum to let him stay. It was the best fun the teenagers had had in a long while, and they had formed a firm friendship group with Dessie, Ben and Lucy. A concerned-looking Sunny took George to one side.

"Look, George, maybe we should let them stay. They will be well guarded here, and the worst of it seems to be over. On the other hand, if they come with us they might be in more danger, and they will definitely be moody and miserable. I'm coming with you and bringing Dita; she's too young to be left here. Please think about it."

A convoy of three vehicles duly arrived in the early evening, and the supplies were gratefully received, along with newspapers, books and news of the outside world. Three burly soldiers were fussed over and shown to their rooms. They had radio equipment that ensured communication would not be a problem. George, Sunny and Dita said goodbye to the two teenage boys, slightly irked at how pleased they were to be left behind.

Wilson gave a more detailed briefing in the Range Rover, describing the audacious kidnap of King Charles, drawing shocked looks and exchanges of concern between George and Sunny. He finished with, "...So you see, we firmly believe that the source of the computer virus that has disabled financial, commercial, and some public websites is located at Devil Gate Drive, and I want you with me when we go in tonight to help identify the principal characters and maybe help with any other problems we may encounter relating to the activities of the APL."

As Dita was happily treated to juice and cakes in an army tent in the woods, George and Sunny were kitted out with uniforms, bulletproof jackets, army boots and night vision goggles. They were instructed to stay close to and always behind the armed and serious Inspector Wilson and PC Jones, their minders for the daring night assault. A pair of night vision binoculars studied them from the woods to the left of their position. Max had seen the arrival of army personnel and the preparations for an assault. He hurried back to The Fox and Hounds to report to Dex, and they would then radio in to their handlers. For the time being their mission was just to observe and report.

DAWN BROKE IN eerie silence at Devil Gate Drive, Hertfordshire country estate of odd-ball APL leader, Peter Morris. An ancient stone wall and electric iron gates fronted onto a single track 'B' road that led to the quaint village of Much Hadham. The estate covered a large wooded area, close to 50,000 acres, with easy access through woods on the three sides away from the front approach. To the rear was a farm track, and it was here that Inspector Wilson assembled his team of armed police. The Army were also there in numbers – SAS soldiers in balaclavas, signals and tactical support units. Three spooks from MI5 made themselves known to the Inspector.

George, Sunny and their minder, PC Jones, hung around outside a hastily erected canteen tent, sipping tea in the chilly darkness, as pale shafts of low sunlight struggled to penetrate through the beech, ash and oak trees. Birds tweeted their morning chorus, a rabbit dived for cover under a bush, adding to a feeling George had that they had been dropped into a timeless, ancient and unspoilt wilderness.

"It's the calm before the storming of the hornet's nest," George remarked, looking around at the hive of activity from eager young soldiers and police officers.

"They're wearing my uniforms," Sunny said, nodding her head towards a huddle of coppers sporting Woolf's Head Security logos on their shoulders.

"Let's hope their training is up to it," George said with a wink and a nudge.

"Come on, it's time for the briefing," Jones interrupted, taking their plastic tea cups and putting them down on a trestle table. She led them out to a grassy clearing where over fifty people had gathered. Inspector Wilson, flanked by a couple of army officers, addressed the group in a serious tone.

"We will approach the house from three sides. The rear, and both sides, but keeping away from the front. There are motion lights which will activate when we step onto the lawn, so that will be our cue to run in and enter the building as quickly as possible through the patio doors and windows you have all be assigned to in the technical briefing. We can expect some armed resistance, and the possibility of tripwire grenades on the lawn, so look for dew on wires, and mark any you see with the flags you've had issued. You all know what to do when you get inside, and the main lounge has been designated as a holding area for captured suspects who must have their hands and feet bound with cable ties."

"One more thing," he added after a short pause. Sporadic murmuring stopped and he had their attention again. "We have tried to keep it under wraps that King Charles is most likely being held hostage in an upstairs bedroom. The army will be responsible for securing his release, and for clearing the upstairs rooms, so my police team should stay out of their way and remain on the ground floor. Our informant has also told us they are about to unleash an internet virus to destabilise commercial activity, so my main focus, in addition to securing their leaders, will be to identify their computer room. Inform me immediately if any of you come across it. Alright, let's get into our start positions, and good luck."

George and Sunny exchanged glances as they put on their padded bullet and blast-proof jackets and helmets. They crept through the woods behind a vigilant PC Jones, taking up their positions in the dark tree line bordering a well-kept dewy lawn. The big grey stone manor house slept. After a few minutes of uncomfortable crouching, Jones waved them forward and they all stepped out in unison, walking at a steady pace across the lawn. They narrowed their eyes as the motion lights came on and they became aware of a buzzing sound above them. *Surely not a swarm of hornets?* George thought, just as he strained to see half a dozen flying objects coming their way from the roof of the house.

"Drones!" Jones shouted, "take cover!" Ripples of gunfire broke out as the drones were identified as hostile threats, some firing machine guns and others dropping cluster bombs on the running invaders. The lawn had suddenly become a battlefield as explosions and gun fire filled the morning air. Windows had opened and shooters fired on the invaders. George and Sunny followed Jones as she dodged past a spray of bullets and urged them to run towards a low brick wall that separated the lawn from a paved patio.

"Stay here and keep your heads down!" Jones commanded as she exchanged machine gun fire with armed defenders shooting from inside the building.

Despite suffering casualties, the assault teams knew the importance of pressing on and gaining quick access. Hostages needed to be rescued and the devilish plans of the APL for more mass destruction neutralised. The drones were soon shot down, and the defenders overcome, as Jones waved at George and Sunny to follow her through patio doors into a large reception room. They stepped gingerly over a bullet-ridden corpse and followed Jones past a line of captives under guard, into the main hall, where Inspector Wilson was waiting for them.

"Come on," he said tersely, "we need to find their computer room and eliminate their computer virus threat." They found a locked door near the back of the house that looked like the entrance to a cellar.

Fighting continued in the hallway as the defenders wrestled with police officers. Wilson guided his charges through the melee, checking the downstairs rooms one by one. Gunshots were heard from upstairs, where the efficient, zero-tolerance SAS were clearing rooms. They were still searching for King Charles, whereas Wilson and his team were out to round up the leaders of the Anti-Poverty League and neutralise the computer virus. Eventually they found a locked room near the back of the house and Wilson called for a burly police officer to break it down. Inside was a staircase that led down to a cellar. A fully-padded officer went first, and received a volley of gunshots for his pains. Wilson pulled the bruised but otherwise unharmed man back and shouted:

"Alright! Throw you weapons down or we'll send down the tear gas! There's no way out. It's over, so give yourselves up!"

After a thirty second wait, they heard a voice shout, "OK, don't shoot, we're coming out!"

"Stay down there, we're coming down!" Wilson detailed two armed officers to precede him and they filed down the narrow staircase. There were three men, one of whom had been the shooter, with an Uzi machine-pistol at his feet and hands on his head. The other two were petrified computer techs, cowering with their hands up behind him. Wilson surveyed with satisfaction the banks of computer equipment along wooden benches, with thick padded foam tiles covering the walls and ceiling, similar to a sound studio.

"This is it," he declared, as they filed in, "their cybercrime centre. Jones, cover their two IT men and the rest of you leave us and take the gunman away to the secure area. And send George and Sunny down here. You two," he said, pointing to the trembling computer men, "sit down. I want to talk to you."

George and Sunny had been hanging around in the corridor, happy that the raid had encountered little opposition. They filed down the narrow staircase to the cellar and joined Wilson as he interrogated the computer techs. "We don't know the passwords," one was saying, "we're just junior computer operators. Only our leaders know how to get into the programme. It's password-protected, honest!" Wilson studied him hard, not convinced he was being told the truth. "Alright, keep them here," he said to PC Jones. "I'll take George and Sunny up to the room where the captives are being held to see if we can identify the leaders. Come on."

They followed Wilson past dozens of armed police and soldiers, some leading prisoners, and were directed to the library where a dozen bleary-eyed suspects were being held. Peter Morris and Stevo were pointed out by Sunny, and a few others she had seen at the recruitment party, but there was no sign of Tommy or Dervla. George and Sunny were particularly pleased to see their former ally-turned-traitor, Stevo, sitting tied to a chair. He managed a cheeky wink to Sunny, but glared with malice at George.

"So you survived the Westminster bombing, but I hear Ken wasn't so lucky." He grinned and continued, "It's too late, the centres of banking and finance have been bombed, and the internet taken down. Capitalism has been dealt a death blow and the world will be a better place for it!"

"How you've changed, Stevo," George said. "Your former army mate, Ken, is alive and recovering, and you haven't dealt a death blow to anyone, just caused a minor inconvenience. But we've dealt a death blow to your crumby organisation."

Wilson needed answers, and separated Morris and Stevo, taking them into different rooms for questioning. They refused to respond to his questions, or identify their computer expert. However, they soon identified Rob Wainwright, from a folder containing photos, names and titles of the group's executive committee. Once confronted he tamely admitted to his involvement. Besides, he looked every inch a computer geek. He was not as strong as the group's leaders, and was meekly led away in the direction of the computer room by Wilson who fully intended to pressurise him into showing them how to disable the internet virus.

In the corridor they were distracted by the sound of cheering and applause coming from upstairs.

"What is it?" Wilson shouted up the grand spiral staircase.

"We've found the king!" A grinning soldier shouted, leaning over the banister. Soldiers and police officers stood back and continued with their applause as a shaken but relieved Charles was helped down the stairs by a female police officer on one arm and a burly soldier in a black balaclava on the other, still wearing a dusty, wrinkled and slightly-torn navy blue suit. He raised a weak smile as he shook hands with Wilson.

"Thank you, Inspector, for this wonderfully daring and timely rescue! Congratulations to all your men and women. You have mine and the nation's thanks!" The soldier supporting him took off his balaclava to the gasps of those around, revealing himself to be Prince Harry. "May I add my thanks to those of my father," he said, slapping Wilson on the shoulder. "I wish you luck, Inspector, with clearing out this nest of vipers and neutralizing the threat." With that he helped his elderly and frail father outside to a waiting car.

"Alright! Excitement over!" Wilson bawled. "Everyone back to work! Let's get every inch of this property searched, there may be people still in hiding; I want all of the prisoners out before the CSIs move in. I'll be down in the cellar if anyone wants me." He pulled Wainwright roughly by the arm and led him to the stairs down to the computer room. The nervous young man was sat down on a swivel chair, sweating profusely and wringing his hands as Wilson and Jones took it in turns to fire questions at him – then Jones mellowed into the voice of reason and they continued to wear him down with a good cop-bad cop routine. He stubbornly refused to give details of the computer virus or the passwords to get onto the system, saying they would kill him if he talked.

George noticed him glance quickly at a drawer, and opened it to reveal a notebook containing scribbled notes and computer coding. There was a string of 1s and 0s, which George recognised as binary code. Binary code is the basic building block of all computer programmes, and George had some experience of computer programming from an ASCII training course he had attended at Railtrack. He knew there are multiple ways of representing letters and symbols to form a binary code. These methods are called encoding.

George addressed Rob directly, "I think these binary strings are part of a computer code, is that right?"

The young man looked glumly down to the floor. "I can't tell you anything – they'll shoot me dead," he said, forlornly.

Wilson stood menacingly over him, hands on hips. "Come on, the game is up...it's only a matter of time before we get in. Any help you give us now will help your case when it comes to court."

George found an ASCII programming book on a shelf and started to leaf through it. He found what he was looking for and said, "The fact that he's got an ASCII book here suggests to me that this is the computer language he has used to design his internet computer bug. ASCII encoding assigns unique binary bytes to 128 different characters. This makes it possible to encode any string of text. Let me have a go at trying to translate this string of binary code on the first page of his notebook..."

George tore a blank page from the notebook and scribbled away with a pen for ten minutes, whilst the others looked on helplessly, hoping that he would come up with something to break the deadlock. George worked from an alphabet chart to decipher the following binary string:

01001000 01100101 01101100 01101100 01101111
00100000 01010111 01101111 01110010 01101100 01100100

Sitting back, he triumphantly announced, "This binary string means, 'Hello World', encoded in ASCII. This might be their password."

Jones snatched the piece of paper from him and tapped furiously away at the computer keyboard. "Yes!...It's worked!" she announced to the group standing around her, as her computer screen sprung to life, with an animated home page showing the words 'Hello World' in melting red letters, hanging over the Houses of Parliament. The mood lightened in the room, and all gathered around the screen as menu options popped up.

"Well done, George!" Wilson patted him on the back. "It'll only be a matter of time now before our IT people identify and dismantle their internet virus. This is your last chance, Wainwright, to help us take down this virus, or you'll be going to prison for a very, very long time...and I'll make sure with no computer access!"

"Oh, alright then, now you're into the system it will only be a matter of time... let me show you." He was wheeled on his chair over to a computer terminal, but remained tied up.

Jones said, "I'll do the typing, just to be on the safe side... you tell me what to do." In a few minutes the virus was disabled, and the police IT section moved in to examine the hard drives and see what other information they could find.

Wilson escorted George and Sunny out into the corridor. "I can't thank you both enough for your help on this. We've never come across such a well-organised, determined and ruthless terrorist group as the Anti-Poverty League. Their name suggests a well-meaning charity group, but they have proved to be anything but. The number of deaths and level of destruction to property, the kidnap of King Charles, and the chaos caused to the finance and banking sectors by their computer virus, has given us a severe wake-up call and nearly brought this country to its knees. Now we can start to repair the damage and get things working again."

They walked out onto the patio and sat on wrought-iron garden chairs. Sunny spoke after a brief silence, "I hope the politicians across the West see this as an opportunity to make reforms to how our societies are run, as clearly there was much public support for the aims of the Anti-Poverty League...although they cleverly disguised their methods until they saw the right signals to strike."

Wilson frowned and said, "Yes, I don't doubt it - they even had sympathy from within the force which I think hampered our investigation. We need to review our security operations as they have gone on their merry way for several months without us knowing much about it. All in all, we've had to fall back on help from you two to crack this thing. It's not over yet – Dervla, Tommy and their accomplices are still at large. But well done again, and I'll be recommending you both for bravery awards. That is, when I get time to write my report."

"And don't forget Ken," George said. "He organised us and had the vision and military expertise to drive the surveillance operation that told us so much about the APL. Poor Ken, betrayed by his ex-army buddy, and badly injured in the Houses of Parliament bombing – he's your real hero."

Wilson had the last word, "You're too modest George, come on I'll drive you to your hotel - we'll be just in time for breakfast."

The dawn chorus started as they crossed the well-kept English country garden, reminding them where they were and that life goes on. Sunny hugged Dita, who was with a female police officer, and they walked to the waiting police Land Cruiser. A strange calm descended on them. George had already turned his mind to a full English breakfast and a mug of steaming tea. "I hope they do black pudding," he said, as they climbed into the car.

CHAPTER FIFTEEN

THEY ADJOURNED TO a pretty little coach house, The Fox and Hounds, tucked away in a leafy village. Sunny hugging her daughter tightly, George stretched and rubbed his stiff left leg, as they shuffled wearily into the breakfast room. A fawning elderly couple offered them fruit juice, cereal, tea and toast. This was enough for Sunny, Dita and PC Jones, but not for George and Wilson; it was the full English breakfast for them – with black pudding and an extra fried egg.

Wilson explained to the owners that they had been up all night and wanted to sleep through the morning. With that, they were all shown to their rooms. Sunny put a tired Dita to bed in a box room connected to their double. Doors closed, Sunny threw her arms around George's neck, drew him towards her and kissed him hard on the lips.

"George, what a clever man you are. I was so impressed with your code-breaking skills. I'm looking forward to us spending some time together, undisturbed..."

"Mmmm, I'm looking forward to it too, but first I'm going to try to call Esther. With all the excitement of the last few days I've not managed to speak to her."

Sunny smiled warmly and said, "That's OK, I want to shower first, you go right ahead."

George turned on his dormant mobile and tapped her name. He was slightly surprised to get a ringing tone, and thought he could hear a phone ringing in the next room. Maybe it's just an echo. There was no answer, so he left a voice message, asking her call him back. He texted her his location for good measure, then put his mobile down, stripped off and headed for the bathroom, joining Sunny in the shower cubicle.

George must have been in a deep sleep, as it took Sunny a few good pushes to wake him up.

"Wake up! There's someone at the door."

George rolled out of bed and pulled on a pair of boxer shorts. A shaft of sunlight pointed the way to the door. On opening it George laughed, as he hugged his teenage daughter, Esther, stunningly stylish in casual dress, but somehow feeling stiff and uneasy.

No sooner had he put his arms around her than two figures emerged from either side of the doorway and pushed them back into the room, shutting the door behind them as George and Esther stumbled but stayed on their feet.

"What the...what's going on?" George blinked as the room was once again darkened. The light switch went on and George recognised the two intruders with horror. Dervla and Tommy. Sunny let out a scream, and Dervla strode towards her, pulling her naked from the bed.

"Hello, my pretty friend," she growled at the struggling woman, "we meet again."

Tommy held a gun and pointed it at George as they locked eyes. "Step away from the girl and get over there," he waved the gun in the direction of a small two-seater sofa on the opposite wall from the bed. George sat down and Sunny was pushed next to him, holding a shirt to cover herself as the terrorists stood gloating over them.

Esther sat on the edge of the bed and, holding her hands to her face, said, "Dad! I'm really shocked to see you here, in the room next to me! These two grabbed hold of me in the corridor…"

Dervla stood, legs apart and hands on hips, menacing in a camouflage jumpsuit, and said, "Alright, enough pleasantries. Not the family reunion you hoped for, is it George? I must admit, it was a bonus finding your daughter here. You two have caused us a lot of trouble, and I hear you were with the police on the raid at the mansion, weren't you?" She leaned forward and bashed their heads together, like a sadistic school teacher.

"Stop it! Leave them alone!" Esther rushed forward, but Tommy pushed her back onto the bed.

"That's enough!" His deep voice added a tone of authority to the proceedings. "Alright, we're taking you with us. Don't cry out or we'll kill you all. Get dressed quickly."

George and Sunny got their clothes on as the unhappy Esther sat fidgeting on the edge of the bed, wondering whether Dex would soon return from his meeting with Max, and what would happen if he did.

Dervla checked the hallway was clear and Tommy pushed them out of the room, towards the fire escape at the back of the building. The skies were grey and there was a light drizzle, making it slippery underfoot as they descended the iron stairs. Dervla led them to a van parked on a track behind the hotel, in a clearing surrounded by trees. As she went to open the sliding door on the side, a crunch of footsteps on twigs made her jerk her head up.

"I don't think you'll be going anywhere with my friends," Dexter growled, holding a pistol. Max stood next to him, pointing a pump-action shotgun at Dervla's midriff.

"Put your hands up and step away from the van," Max said, in a calm voice that suggested he had prior experience. Dervla, knowing an armed Tommy was behind her crouched inside the van, dropped to the ground, and Tommy fired at the two men. Dex and Max dived in opposite directions as bullets whizzed by. Dervla drew her automatic and Tommy stepped out, standing menacingly over the Americans sprawled on the forest floor amongst the twigs.

"Don't move! Armed police!" The loud, authoritative voice of Inspector Wilson boomed across the forest clearing. "Put your hands up where I can see them!"

Tommy whirled around and pointed his revolver at a police officer. Two shots rang out, within seconds of each other, and both the police officer and Tommy fell to the ground, in a slow motion synchronised crumple.

The women screamed, and Dervla made a run for it. But PC Jones had been waiting for this moment ever since police training academy, and sprinted after her, bringing her down with a well-executed rugby tackle. George, Sunny and Esther peeped out of the open van doorway and saw a flurry of movement as armed police rushed in to help the two stunned Americans and make sure Tommy was neutralised. Inspector Wilson appeared and stood in front of them. Tommy groaned to show he was still alive, clutching a bloody gunshot wound in his shoulder, and the shot police offer was helped slowly to his feet, dusting off the front of his bulletproof jacket, and bending to pick up the bullet that would become a prized keepsake.

"Here, it's safe to come out now," he said, helping them out of the van one by one.

The two couples hugged, realizing they had survived a near-death moment. They looked on in silence as a handcuffed Dervla was led away. Tommy was helped to his feet and taken to a separate police van.

"These two are so dangerous that they'll be kept apart and well guarded," Wilson explained.

Wilson escorted them back to the pub where Sunny found her daughter still fast asleep in bed, none-the-wiser for the dramatic events that had just unfolded. They all took seats in the lounge, looking to Wilson to lead the conversation.

He eyed Dex and Max critically, and said, "I was aware that the CIA were observing from a distance but I was unprepared for any direct involvement. You both nearly got killed out there."

"He's not CIA!" Essie cried out, "He's just a student on holiday!" She squeezed Dex's arm.

"I know who he is," Wilson said. "My MI5 colleagues have briefed me on his family connections to the CIA, and your driver, 'Max', is one of their European operatives. Our security services have been monitoring their movements."

Dex opened his mouth but quickly closed it. He couldn't think of anything productive to say. Wilson gave him a disapproving look before turning to George and Sunny, "We saw them coming in through the fire escape, but chose to wait until they left before tackling them. Sorry for the scare you experienced, but there was no other way. At least we stopped them before they got away, and thank God, none of you were hurt."

George, unimpressed at them being deemed expendable hostages, chose to keep his thoughts to himself. Relief was his primary feeling, and he put his sore arms around both Essie and Sunny.

"I hope that's an end to it. I don't think I can handle any more excitement." He kissed the two women on their foreheads and said to the Inspector, "This is my daughter,

Esther, in case you haven't worked it out. She's been dating Dexter, who came over to Windsor to meet Derrick and myself, and I had no idea they were here. I was unaware that Dexter is a CIA operative, until now. She met him at Harvard University on an exchange visit. Now I don't know what to believe."

George turned to Dex and asked, "Is dating my daughter just part of your spy cover story or do you have genuine feelings for her?"

"Of course I have feelings for her," Dex quickly replied, "and I didn't target her as part of a cover story. When I met her I wasn't involved in this, or anything for that matter. I was just studying for a degree like all other students, and not yet a fully operational agent. It was the CIA who saw an opportunity to exploit my relationship with your daughter, Sir, honest." He gazed into Essie's eyes and squeezed her hands. "I hope you believe me, sweetheart, I'm in love with you." She gulped and a tear came to her eye. She put her arms around his neck and kissed him.

"Well, that clears that up," George said. "Inspector, I hope you won't be charging him with anything?"

Wilson held up his hands, "It's in the hands of MI5, and they may want a word with the pair of them. I won't be detaining them. For my part, I'm prepared to accept that this was a covert observation mission from our cousins across the sea, and they did help by confronting the two suspects and drawing them out into the open where we were able to apprehend them. It will all go in my report. Hopefully, that's an end to it, and we have all their leaders now in custody. I'm needed elsewhere. You're all free to go. George and Sunny, I've made a car available to drive you back to the guesthouse you were staying at to be with your boys and other friends."

"I'm not leaving without coffee and some nice home-made scones with jam and butter," George said.

Sunny hugged his arm and purred, "You are the undisputed master of understatement."

Esther brightened up and quipped, "I'd just say he's the master of modesty!" They all laughed and relaxed, each quietly reflecting on the violent shoot-out they were drawn into that must have lasted less than a minute. George let out a huge sigh of relief, drawing laughter from the group. A smile cracked his lips as he gazed with devotion at Essie and Sunny; a proud father, loving partner and finally, maybe, a contented bird-watching retiree.

CHAPTER SIXTEEN

THE NEIGHBOURS CRANED their necks and huddled in gossiping groups as a fleet of three black, shiny cars, with royal standards fluttering on their bonnets, drew up in front of George's council flat. Sunny, George, Ken, Esther, Derrick, Ravi and Dita were all waiting, dressed in their smartest clothes, excited at the prospect of being the invited guests of King Charles III at Windsor Castle. A royal page, dressed in the finest livery, walked to his front door, and presented George with a gilt-edged envelope. He took his time opening it, turning it over in his hands as he stood on the doorstep, surveying the gallery of nosy neighbours.

"I shall be delighted to accept his Royal Highness's invitation to tea in the state rooms at Windsor Castle," he announced, perhaps louder than was necessary. They filed out of the front door and arranged themselves in the back of the largest of the cars – a stretched Bentley with two rows of soft leather seats facing each other. Ken had discarded his crutches and managed with a walking stick. He turned to George and said, "This is a proud moment for me, George, having served in the King's Regiment. Technically, I'm being decorated for bravery by my former commander-in-chief."

The motorcade drove through the imposing gates to Windsor Castle, past flag-waving monarchists, and into the lower courtyard, coming to a halt outside the imposing Saint George's Chapel. From here, they were required to walk uphill, past the Round Tower, to the State Apartments. Here they were greeted by a royal page, who guided them to the Garter Throne Room, where a table had been laid for tea, before an impressive royal throne. They took their seats whilst admiring the coats-of-arms of knights of the Order of the Garter around the room.

"The Most Noble Order of the Garter was founded in 1348," their host explained. "It is the highest order of chivalry, and the third most prestigious honour after the Victoria Cross and George Cross, in the United Kingdom."

"You will not be invited to become Knights of the Order of the Garter, as membership is restricted to the Sovereign, the Prince of Wales, and twenty-four living companions. This quota is currently full, and it is a case of 'dead men's shoes', as it were, to be invited to join the order." This was intended as a joke, and a broad smile gave them the cue for polite laughter. They were certainly all out of their comfort zones in such an imposing, regal setting.

"Tea will now be served, and the royal party will join you shortly."

George raised his hand, as if at school. "Erm, my invitation says I'll be receiving the George Cross, for gallantry in the face of the enemy, along with my colleague, Ken. Can you tell us something about this award?"

"Why yes, indeed," the middle-aged male page clasped his hands together, as if he had been waiting for such a question. "The George Cross was instituted by our king's grandfather, King George VI, in 1940, and is the highest award for civilians who demonstrate extreme bravery, often in the face of an enemy in a war situation. The citation is for George Osborne and Kenneth Jones for their gallant and unselfish actions in preventing the destruction of the Houses of Parliament." He stood smiling and George blushed with pride.

He turned to Sunny and squeezed her hand, "I'm sorry you were left out, love, you should be getting a medal as well, as a surviving member of the Thames Valley Defence Force."

"Medals are for boys," she said, kissing him lightly on the cheek.

"Three cheers for Ken and Dad!" Essie said, lifting her bone china tea cup. "Hip, hip, horray!"

A door opened behind the throne and a uniformed page banged a golden rod on the floor. "His Majesty, King Charles the Third, and His Royal Highness Prince Henry of Wales!" The king and Prince Harry entered, wearing smart suits, looking like they were attending a business meeting. They were invited to form a line and shake hands, bowing slightly in deference. Essie attempted an awkward curtsey, at which Derrick giggled and pushed her. They were then invited to stand by their chairs until Charles and Harry had sat, jointly at the head of the table, before they took their seats.

Ceremony over, King Charles pulled his cuffs in trademark fashion and said, rather pointlessly, "Please, let's not stand on ceremony." He beamed at the assembled group and turned to George and Ken, sitting to his left. "Ah, I vaguely recognise you two from your photos on the citation documents. Welcome, George and Ken, and thanks for your sterling efforts in thwarting those dastardly terrorists! Please, finish your tea and cakes, and we'll start in about ten minutes."

As the king and prince were served tea and cakes, Essie, who found herself sitting next to Prince Harry, started a whispered conversation with him. Ken was aching to ask Charles about the current political situation in the country and what his plans were, but had been warned by the page as part of their etiquette briefing not to address the monarch unless he first talks to you. Nevertheless, Ken kept an eye on the chewing monarch, hoping to catch his eye and draw him into conversation. After half a minute, it happened.

"Erm, Ken, you were formerly an officer in my regiment, is that right?"

"Yes, Your Majesty. I was a captain in the King's and did three tours overseas," he quickly replied. "May I ask, are you fully recovered from your ordeal? It must have been a terrifying experience..."

A page stepped forward, but Charles held up his hand. "That's alright. Thank you for asking, yes. It was all a frightful shock, and I took a few days off to be with my family and get over it. Back to business now."

Ken saw his chance to probe. "And, if I may be so bold, what are your immediate plans? I mean, the country is anxious to know the way forward..."

Silence had fallen around the table, as all conversations stopped and everyone listened in, half expecting a royal rebuke.

Charles eyed him and considered his response. "Yes, well I've come to realise, over the past few days, that expediency is required on my part. The country, as you rightly point out, is holding its collective breath, waiting to hear what this interim government, of which I'm head, will come up with. After the kidnap incident, I'm more acutely aware of the dangers of a political vacuum, and the fact that there are malevolent groups who wish to take advantage and further destabilise us to the point of anarchy and no doubt revolution. The country has been here before, at the time of Oliver Cromwell, when my predecessor, the unfortunate King Charles I, had his head cut off. I don't wish to suffer the same fate, and so have resolved to make public the plans drawn up by my Privy Council to move the country swiftly towards a new constitution and democratic elections."

There was a ripple of applause from around the table at this welcome news.

King Charles wasn't finished. "I feel a strong sense of destiny, and I'm not going to let this opportunity to govern pass without injecting some of my ideas into the national sphere, as it were. When I roll out the roadmap to democracy, expect some interesting, some might say controversial, policy announcements, which I believe will be for the public good."

He sat back, an enigmatic smile playing on his worn face, whilst they were all left wondering what these policies might be. "Now, let's get on with the ceremony, shall we?"

AUTHOR'S NOTE

This is my first novel, and was two years in the writing. The story started as a weekly fiction blog on *wordpress.com* under the title, *Life of George*. I then took it down from my blog site and worked it into chapters, adding new material including the Essie and Dex relationship sub-plot. I then sent the manuscript for proofing and copyediting, before solicited for beta readers to give feedback.

I must thank my proof reader/copy editor, Sinead Fitzgibbon (@sfitzgib), for her patience and advice in guiding me to the final version. I must also thank half a dozen beta readers who read and commented with enthusiasm. Many of their suggestions have been included to firm-up plot and character development, dialogue and iron out inconsistencies. Finally, I designed a rough-and-ready book cover concept and then sent it to be professionally re-created by a graphic designer found through *fiverr.com*.

For more about the author please visit my author page and website and engage with me on social media:

Author page: http://Author.to/timwalkerwrites

Follow me on Twitter: @timwalker1666

Facebook Page: http://www.facebook.com/timwalkerwrites

See my blog: http://tnwalker.wordpress.com

...and visit my website: http://timwalkerwrites.co.uk

21682077R00104

Printed in Great Britain
by Amazon